The Doom of the Great City; Being the Narrative
of a Survivor, Written A.D. 1942

The Doom of the Great City;

Being the Narrative of a Survivor, Written A.D. 1942

WILLIAM DELISLE HAY

Edited by Michael Kramp and Sarita Jayanty Mizin

WEST VIRGINIA UNIVERSITY PRESS
MORGANTOWN

ISBN 978-1-959000-37-2 (paperback) / 978-1-959000-38-9 (ebook)

Library of Congress Cataloging-in-Publication Data

Names: Hay, W. Delisle (William Delisle), 1851- author. | Kramp, Michael, editor. |
    Mizin, Sarita Jayanty, editor.
Title: The doom of the great city : being the narrative of a survivor; written A.D. 1942 /
    by William Delisle Hay ; edited by Michael Kramp and Sarita Jayanty Mizin.
Description: First edition. | Morgantown : West Virginia University Press, 2025. |
    Series: Salvaging the anthropocene; book 4 | Includes bibliographical references |
    Identifiers: LCCN 2024038416 | ISBN 9781959000372 (paperback) |
    ISBN 9781959000389 (ebook) Subjects: LCGFT: Science fiction. | Novels.
Classification: LCC PR4765.H93 D66 2025 | DDC 823/.8—dc23/eng/20241011
LC record available at https://lccn.loc.gov/2024038416

Cover image: Engraved drawing by William Small, "A November Fog in London,"
1877. Penta Springs Limited /Alamy Stock Photo
Book and cover design by Than Saffel / WVU Press

For our students

CONTENTS

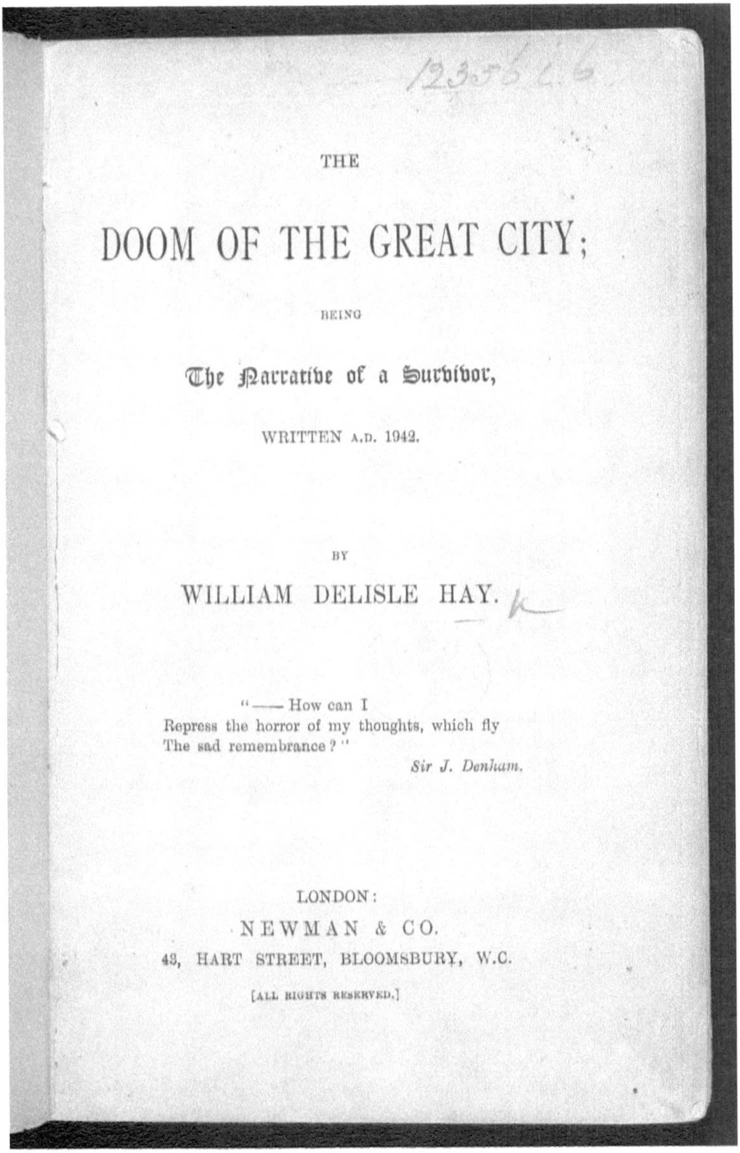

THE

DOOM OF THE GREAT CITY;

BEING

𝔗𝔥𝔢 𝔑𝔞𝔯𝔯𝔞𝔱𝔦𝔳𝔢 𝔬𝔣 𝔞 𝔖𝔲𝔯𝔳𝔦𝔳𝔬𝔯,

WRITTEN A.D. 1942.

BY

WILLIAM DELISLE HAY.

"—— How can I
Repress the horror of my thoughts, which fly
The sad remembrance?"

Sir J. Denham.

LONDON:

NEWMAN & CO.

43, HART STREET, BLOOMSBURY, W.C.

Figure 1. Title page from *The Doom of the Great City*, first edition (1880).
(The British Library 12356.i.6. Reproduced with permission.)

Figure 2. Cover image from William Delisle Hay, *The Doom of the Great City*, first edition (1880). (The British Library 12356.i.6. Reproduced with permission.)

ACKNOWLEDGMENTS

We are sincerely grateful for the expert guidance and support of Derek Krissoff, Sarah Munroe, Natalie Homer, Kristen Bettcher, and everyone at West Virginia University Press. In addition, we are thankful for the financial support of Lehigh University's Office of Research, including funding for archival research and manuscript preparation. We would also like to thank the University of Wisconsin–Eau Claire's English department and Office of Research and Sponsored Programs, which provided funding for time reassignment and research materials. We greatly appreciate the anonymous reviewers who provided valuable feedback and recommendations for revisions.

For each of us, this was our first foray into collaborative scholarship, and as Deleuze and Guattari note in their introduction to *A Thousand Plateaus*, "Since each of us was several, there was already quite a crowd." We are truly grateful to each other for the chance to do this work and learn together. We hope that our work makes this novella more accessible to a variety of audiences. May critical engagement with such texts no longer be limited to those who would have always been able to find them.

We would like to thank our colleagues, students, and friends, who continue to challenge us to pursue new kinds of intellectual activity and thinking. This is part of the work. Our conversations matter.

Finally, we would like to thank our families and especially our parents, without whom none of this would be possible.

NOTE ON THE TEXT

The Doom of the Great City was published in 1880 by Newman & Co. publishers in Bloomsbury. We have worked with the text of this first publication for our critical edition and maintained all original spelling and style. This edition of the text includes some original notes from the author, which we have identified in the footnotes to distinguish them from our own annotations.

INTRODUCTION

Michael Kramp and Sarita Jayanty Mizin

Evil!—one seemed to see it everywhere. In those latter days there had been past years of terribly bad weather, destroying harvests, and adding to the iniquity of the land-system of the country a very close cause of distress for all agriculturists; there had been long and severe depression in trade, augmented by the fact that the manufacturing industry of the country was fast going from her, owing to want of public spirit and the avaricious selfishness that had supplanted the old British feeling, owing also to continual strife between capital and labour. Such distress as was then felt throughout the rural districts of the United Kingdom had seldom before been equalled; it reacted upon the urban populations, and peculiarly on that of London; every profession, trade, or mode of earning money was over-crowded in its ranks and was curtailed in its action; while, if positive destitution overtook the already existing poor, it also touched ranks that had been heretofore far removed from its approach; extensive emigration palliated but could not cure the disease; and the piteous efforts of the thousands who were struggling with adversity in manifold paths of life were something sad to see, sad to remember.

—William Delisle Hay, *The Doom of the Great City*

The colonist makes history and he knows it.
　　　　　—Frantz Fanon, *The Wretched of the Earth*

The world will surely end, but that won't necessarily be the end of
our troubles.
　　　　　—Alenka Zupančič, "The End of Ideology,
　　　　　the Ideology of the End"

William Delisle Hay's *The Doom of the Great City* (1880) recounts the swift devastation of London: an immense fog envelops the capital, incapacitates its modern systems of transport and communication, generates tremendous confusion and fear, and quickly annihilates the urban population. The dramatic demise of the metropolis, however, is neither sudden nor simple; it is at once the result of industrial capitalism, imperial networks, discernible climatic change, and the "Evil!" that "one seemed to see . . . everywhere" (88). The narrator, one of the few survivors of the cataclysmic event, details failed civic institutions, labor strife, the imprudent conduct of London's inhabitants, and acts of settler colonialism that produce decadence and destruction. He also explicitly dates the disaster to 1882, two years after the novella's publication, and narrates his story in 1942, pushing the narrative forward in time. The novella imaginatively condenses a chain of anthropocenic effects—economic, social, racist, and ecological—into a single man's account and functions both as a fictional history and a herald of one possible, terrible future.

The Doom of the Great City contributes to numerous late nineteenth-century discourses about imminent cultural dangers:

ecological exigencies, such as global warming and the perils of industrialization, overcrowded cities, and extractivism; economic worries tied to evolving imperial markets and the dwindling countryside; and broader anxieties about national, moral, and racial degeneration. While Hay's tale operates, at times, as a righteous jeremiad about London that laments the corruption and debauchery of the city, the narrator's memoir accomplishes diverse literary, cultural, and political work. It details the ruin of the capital but the cataclysm apparently leaves the rest of the world unscathed. It depicts the horrors of an environmental catastrophe but does little to raise alarm about its causes or outline meaningful solutions. It chronicles tremendous death, despair, even terror. Still, the storyteller, who relocates to scenic Māori land on the North Island of New Zealand (Te Ika-a-Māui), repeatedly notes his pleasures as a colonizer, contributing to the repopulation of a region while displacing Indigenous peoples. At the same time, *The Doom of the Great City* points to many of the hazards of the "major and still growing impacts of human activities on earth and atmosphere" that we now designate as defining conditions of the Anthropocene, and Hay specifically illustrates the strategic deployment of such hazards that we continue to observe in both fictional literature and government policies.[1] His narrator promises to "marshall [his]

1. Paul J. Crutzen and Eugene F. Stoermer, "The Anthropocene," in *The Future of Nature: Documents of Global Change*, ed. Libby Robin, Sverker Sörlin, and Paul Warde (New Haven: Yale University Press, 2013), 484. Elizabeth Povinelli, in *Geontologies: A Requiem to Late Liberalism*, notes that the Anthropocene concept itself "is as much a product of the coalfields

recollections," modeling how pronouncements of ecological crises might achieve multiple ends, even the ends of white supremacy (74).

We have compiled this critical edition of Hay's story of urban apocalypse in a time of ecological, economic, and social crises—and organized responses to such crises. As we endure the dire and tangible consequences of the Anthropocene, such as climate emergencies, dwindling natural resources, and industrial pollution that, as Hay forecast, have produced "years of terribly bad weather, destroying harvests," we also witness the rise of worldwide movements confronting global warming, racial injustice, fascist leaders, hunger and homelessness, and sexual violence (88). During this tumultuous period, Indigenous, postcolonial, and Black feminist scholars have clarified the limitations, imperialist frameworks, and racist presumptions of the Anthropocene as an intellectual concept for understanding history, explaining geography, and rationalizing settler colonialism, often drawing on the pioneering work of Frantz Fanon. Māori scholar Linda Tuhiwai Smith, for example, addresses the far-reaching ramifications of creative, scientific, and policy-based anthropogenic studies and notes how "many researchers, academics and project workers may see the benefits of their particular research projects as serving a greater good 'for mankind'" but concludes that "Indigenous peoples across the world have other stories to tell which not only question the

as an analysis of their formation" (Durham, NC: Duke University Press, 2016), 10.

assumed nature of those ideals and the practices that they generate, but also serve to tell an alternative story: the history of Western research through the eyes of the colonized."[2] Tuhiwai Smith urges us to listen for such stories, which have often been silenced—stories that complicate pronouncements of Western progress or revival. *The Doom of the Great City* is a story that legitimates the losses of Indigenous peoples as part of ongoing anthropocenic processes—if we are prepared to listen.

Gaia Giuliani, Katherine McKittrick, Tiffany Lethabo King, Kathryn Yusoff, Lisa Lowe, Elizabeth Povinelli, and others have drawn on the work of Fanon, Indigenous scholars such as Tuhiwai Smith, and Black feminist thinkers Sylvia Wynter, Audre Lorde, and bell hooks to indict what Giuliani refers to as the "logics of the Anthropocene" as "a set of principles based on ontologies of exploitation, extermination and natural resource exhaustion." Giuliani concludes, "Such principles are indiscriminately applied to organic and inorganic life through a panoply of 'technologies of power' serving the Anthropocenic order of things and determining who is worthy of benefiting from value extraction and being saved from the catastrophe (the 'we') and who is expendable."[3] This critical dialogue between postcolonial and decolonial thinkers, Indigenous scholars, and Black feminist theorists informs our editorial

2. Linda Tuhiwai Smith, *Decolonizing Methodologies: Research and Indigenous Peoples* (London: Zed Books, 2012), 2.
3. Gaia Giuliani, *Monsters, Catastrophes, and the Anthropocene: A Postcolonial Critique* (London: Routledge, 2021), 6.

work as we discuss the local and global effects of *The Doom of the Great City* as well as its historical and future contexts.[4] As Giuliani argues, narratives of calamity maintain great utility for modern cultures because they invoke "a shared history and a common future," justify drastic and damaging actions on a global scale, and reify "logics" that exploit, deplete, and exterminate designated lands and peoples.[5] *The Doom of the Great City* offers a haunting late-Victorian example of this literary practice, fulfilling Alenka Zupančič's prognosis that "the world will surely end, but that won't necessarily be the end of our troubles."[6] Hay's story illustrates how the versatility of apocalyptic stories validates select anthropocenic desolations, yet even select desolations do not delimit the damage to the past, present, and futures of non-Western lands and Indigenous peoples.

4. Porscha Fermanis provides a useful contemporary example of how speculative and utopian literature continue to be used to advance white supremacist narratives and subnarratives. Fermanis explores the legacy of Samuel Butler's *Erewhon*, including its contribution to "the dispossessive and eliminationist imprint of what has been called 'settler utopianism'" that "promoted New Zealand as an idyllic, preindustrialized, and land-rich double of the original island nation." Fermanis specifically examines whether Butler's settler-colonial treatment of "a racialized form of White dispossessive utopianism . . . offers a profitable way of contextualizing Brexit's regressive-progressive ideology and its promise of future plentitude and fulfilment," which she ties directly to "its dreams of a transcontinental pure White race" (92). See Porscha Fermanis, "Brexit, *Erewhon*, and Utopia," *Historical Reflections*, 47, no. 2 (Summer 2021): 91–104.

5. Giuliani, *Monsters*, 5.

6. Alenka Zupančič, "The End of Ideology, the Ideology of the End," *South Atlantic Quarterly* 119, no. 4 (2020): 844.

The Doom of the Great City displays anthropocenic logic within local, global, and historical contexts. The narrator recalls how nineteenth-century industrialization, urbanization, and pollution beget the deadly fog, but he also mourns what he presents as a lost cultural order—"the want of public spirit and the avaricious selfishness that had supplanted the old British feeling." He memorializes an atrophying British people in need of revival. We learn of "[S]uch distress as was then felt throughout the rural districts of the United Kingdom [that] had seldom before been equalled" (88–89). The destruction of London may appear precipitous, but the narrator seemingly sanctions the eradication of the capital by itemizing corrupt economic, legal, religious, and social institutions; he, in turn, enjoys prosperity and pleasures in the lands of the Māori people.[7] In *The Doom of the Great City*, Hay adopts anthropocenic logic, decimating the English capital *and* acting with the privilege of a Victorian imperialist, anticipating Fanon's terse declaration that "the colonist makes history and he knows it."[8] He renders the collapse of a global metropolis as a triumphant parable: an individual prevails over extreme adversity, writes his own version of the event,

7. In *Memories of Empire*, vol. 1, *The White Man's World* (Oxford: Oxford University Press, 2011), Bill Schwarz points to something of the versatility of apocalyptic rhetoric to advance white supremacist and xenophobic projects with an extensive analysis of Enoch Powell's 1968 "Rivers of Blood" speech, in which the former conservative politician adopts hyperbolic language and dramatic imagery to criticize immigration to the United Kingdom and the proposed Race Relations Bill. See specifically 33–40.
8. Frantz Fanon, *The Wretched of the Earth* (New York: Grove Press, 2004), 15.

and transmits this history to his present and future progeny from the comforts of a colonized New Zealand.

THE VICTORIAN ANTHROPOGENIC EVENT AS A GLOBAL EVENT

Researchers of the Anthropocene study the worldwide consequences of human-directed phenomena, including industrialization, urbanization, resource extraction, imperialism, and slavery. Scholars such as Elizabeth Carolyn Miller, Jesse Oak Taylor, Eva Horn, Maura Coughlin, Nathan Hensley, Wendy Parkins, Philip Steer, Cara New Daggett, and Barri J. Gold have observed the importance of cultural developments in climate science, geology, energy, the slave trade, and colonial exploitation in British literature and art of the 1800s, helping us to discern early markers of the Anthropocene that we might dismiss or otherwise ignore. They have also encouraged us to study Victorian writers alongside prominent scientific, medical, and naturalist texts like Charles Lyell's *Principles of Geology* (1830–33), George Perkins Marsh's *Man and Nature* (1864), Luke Howard's early climatological works, and Svante Arrhenius's groundbreaking studies on global warming. While many still debate the origins of the Anthropocene, Daggett suggests "it is arguably the Victorian period when humans first began to sense that these effects might be planetary and truly catastrophic."[9]

9. Cara New Daggett, *The Birth of Energy: Fossil Fuels, Thermodynamics, and the Politics of Work* (Durham: Duke University Press, 2019), 9.

Nineteenth-century thinkers recognized the possible global implications of human activities, but this incipient knowledge, as Kyle Whyte notes, most assuredly did not stall "colonialism and capitalism," what he identifies as "the groundwork for industrialization and militarization—or carbon-intensive economics—which produce the drivers of anthropogenic climate change." Imperialism, extraction economics, and violent exploitations persisted—and persist. As Whyte concludes, "The colonial invasion that began centuries ago caused anthropogenic environmental changes that rapidly disrupted many Indigenous peoples, including deforestation, pollution, modification of hydrological cycles, and the amplification of soil-use and terraforming for particular types of farming, grazing, transportation, and residential, commercial and government infrastructure."[10] Hay documents such global ramifications, connecting the disaster in London with the impacts of his narrator's resettlement on Māori lands in New Zealand, but he also invites us to ignore this planetary peril. The invitation to ignore or erase is key to the continuity of systems of "racialized capitalism" that Yusoff describes as structuring "experience from the vantage point of Western colonialism and its ongoing colonial present."[11] *The Doom of the Great City* does not depict the British Empire, its patrons, or its networks of resource exhaustion

10. Kyle Whyte, "Indigenous Climate Change Studies: Indigenizing Futures, Decolonizing the Anthropocene," *English Language Notes* 55, nos. 1–2 (2017): 154.
11. Kathryn Yusoff, *A Billion Black Anthropocenes or None* (Minneapolis: University of Minnesota Press, 2018), 60.

as explicit threats to Indigenous communities, and neither does it describe how the empire was built through the unfree labor of colonized subjects. The Māori are simply absent from the text, as are the forms of coerced and indentured labor that supported a settler empire in Hay's pastoral narrative.[12]

Hay's frame story, set in Taupō on the North Island, allows him to relate a tale of modern urban apocalypse from a site of distant pastoral comfort, and despite his colonial zeal, he (perhaps unintentionally) mentions the ecological effects of imperialism across time and space. The narrator of *The Doom of the Great City* remembers how he came to this Māori land "so many years ago—came to what was then almost a solitude." He admires New Zealand's natural splendor and supposed seclusion and acknowledges how his arrival contributes to the adulteration of the island's "virgin wilderness," remarking that the area in which he has lived for "many years" has become "one of our most populous rural districts" (73). Indigenous, postcolonial, and Anthropocene scholars have made clear how Western tourism, immigration, economic policies, political campaigns, research, and imperial ventures of the past three

12. See, in particular, the narrator's ambiguous early comments regarding the evening of his birthday celebration: "At dinner, after they had drunk my health and I had responded, it was little Laura who stood up and proposed the toast of 'Our absent friends, all round Lake Taupo,'—which I need not say was drunk enthusiastically. But I will not go further into these details, for I have set myself to write about another and far different subject" (4). We do not know the identities of "Our absent friends, all round Lake Taupo" and Hay may be referencing "absent" Māori persons before affirming his intention to "write about another and far different subject."

hundred years have disproportionately damaged—even obliterated—non-Western peoples of color. Mike Davis's landmark study, *Late Victorian Holocausts: El Niño Famines and the Making of the Third World*, specifically delineates how Britain's global enterprises contributed to "the emergence of a 'third world' and its vulnerability to extreme climate events."[13] He writes, "What seemed from a metropolitan perspective the nineteenth century's final blaze of imperial glory was, from an Asian or African viewpoint, only the hideous light of a giant funeral pyre."[14] Davis lays bare the planetary effects of British industrialism and imperialism, the ongoing legacies of plantation slavery and the slave trade, and the dangers of changing weather patterns for food production and attendant climatic emergencies. At a vital point in Hay's plot, the narrator signals such expansive possibilities when he muses, "[I]f the fog could attain to such virulence over any special locality, there was no just reason for supposing that its area of destructive maleficence might not be enlarged to an almost indefinite extent" (105). The novella's late nineteenth-century assessment of a local atmospheric event suggests global implications, but the narrator fails to explore these implications because, as Tuhiwai Smith notes, colonizers' perspectives regularly silence Indigenous stories, including their stories of the Anthropocene. When we discern this process in Hay's fiction, we become

13. Mike Davis, *Late Victorian Holocausts: El Niño Famines and the Making of the Third World* (London: Verso, 2001), 328.
14. Davis, *Late Victorian Holocausts*, 8.

more attuned to these enduring acts of silencing and extermination elsewhere.

The spectacular, local storyline of *The Doom of the Great City* may entice some readers to dismiss its imperial framing, but Hay's calculated representations of nature and "the natural" underline the global ramifications of his tale of ecological disaster. His narrator repeatedly claims that the dissolute people of London display altered conceptions of nature and, by extension, British culture: "[T]hey worshipped beauty, but it was not the beauty of created Nature, but that of art—and such art!" (83). He sharply derides the licentious inhabitants of the capital for reveling in the luxuries of late Victorian urban life—a critique he replicates in his white supremacist narrative, *Three Hundred Years Hence* (1881)—and he often portrays the deadly fog as a focused punishment for "the black enormity of London sin" that "was foul and rotten to the very core, and steeped in sin of every imaginable variety" (79–80). The novella highlights the vices of late Victorian society, laments a lost agrarian population, and celebrates "the sweet pastoral quiet of" the narrator's deceased "father's pleasant rural vicarage," akin to the serenity of his New Zealand retirement (76). Hay's veneration of "natural" living serves to endorse a vanishing rural tradition and a white British people that the narrator fears are disappearing amid modernity—but who somehow thrive in the Māori lands surrounding Lake Taupō and throughout the Empire. The residents of the English capital have eschewed simple, rural lives in favor of an artificial, decadent, urban existence. And this transformation does not doom just one city; it requires global networks of extractivism to fuel industrialization and maintain the indulgences of late Victorian urban society, the very features of modernity that precipitate the apocalyptic fog, prompting the narrator to seek out a new home far from England. Hay's fiction imagines a limitless nature ripe for imperialist extraction and his narrator's prolific family—all suggestive of Western narratives that, according to Tuhiwai Smith, derive from settler-colonialists' "fanciful, ill-informed opinions" that today are "taken for granted as facts" and continue to impact non-Indigenous peoples' attitudes toward Indigenous lands and peoples.[15] *The Doom of the Great City* dramatizes a fabulous apocalyptic event that may appear finite, but the narrative underscores the global complications of London's demise and reminds us why writers of speculative fiction often convey white supremacist responses to ecological crises.

HAY AND THE VICTORIAN CULTURAL DEPLOYMENT OF NEW ZEALAND

The Doom of the Great City represents many of the ecological consequences of British modernity and the effects of these consequences on both Western and non-Western peoples and lands. The narrator's frame story sketches his life in New Zealand, gestures toward the far-reaching impacts of his activities, and alludes to Hay's own time in the former colony. As both a fellow of the Royal Geographical Society and a mycologist,

15. Tuhiwai Smith, *Decolonizing Methodologies*, 82.

Hay traveled extensively throughout the British Empire. His semi-autobiographical work, *Brighter Britain! Or, Settler and Maori in Northern New Zealand,* champions the global influences of Victorian imperialism. In his preface, he asserts, "I am not an emigration-tout, a land-salesman, or a tourist. When I went to New Zealand I went there as an emigrant. . . . I have, therefore, written from the point of view of a settler."[16] Hay identifies himself not as a brief visitor or mercenary business-man but as a settler-colonist. The narrator of *The Doom of the Great City* uses similar language to describe his post-fog retirement, insisting he is "still hale and hearty" and quickly adding, "[H]ow could it be otherwise, living as I do in the most beautiful climate of the world" (72). Hay presents his nostalgic story-teller as a worthy survivor and a remarkable paternal figure, encircled by rural delights and endowed with children and grandchildren scattered throughout the empire. We learn nothing of his spouse; instead, the New Zealand environment seemingly facilitates the proliferation of the narrator's descendants: "And what a family it is, to be sure. . . . There were no less than forty-three of them, old and young, big and little, who came to bid 'Grandfather' good morning to-day, and to wish him all the customary felicitations; and then, too, what a pile of letters have I had from all of you who are at a distance in your various homes scattered over Australasia!" (72). He begins his tale by

---

16. William Delisle Hay, *Brighter Britain! Or, Settler and Maori in Northern New Zealand*, 2 vols. (London: Richard Bentley and Son, 1882), 1:iii.

relishing his extensive lineage, rekindled on Indigenous lands, marked by wondrous weather, far removed from the toxic fog.

In *Brighter Britain!*, Hay discusses the ostensible benefits of imperialism, the natural grandeur of New Zealand that informs *The Doom of the Great City*, and nineteenth-century cultural understandings of Māori people and land developed by British writers such as Thomas Macaulay, Samuel Butler, and Sir George Grey, twice appointed the colony's governor. While observing Auckland, Hay reports "on the shaggy shores of Britain's under-world, in the very heart of recent Maori-dom, so . . . far removed from the tracks of ancient civilization," and claims, "[W]e look around us and are filled with wonder and a feeling akin to awe. This is what colonization means; this is the work of colonists; this is the evidence of energy that may well seem titanic, or industry that appears herculean; this is Progress!"[17] For Hay, British settler-colonialism has not caused ecological devastation or climate emergencies; it has, instead, accomplished wonders, replacing "Maori-dom" through "the work of colonists," "industry that appears herculean," and the eradication of Indigenous peoples framed as "Progress!"[18] Hay's

17. Hay, *Brighter Britain!* 1:19.
18. Hay's description of colonial progress references widespread cultural discourses that treated New Zealand as "Better Britain" or "Greater Britain." For an extensive discussion of these related but different discourses, see James Belich's historical study, *Making Peoples: A History of the New Zealanders, from Polynesian Settlement to the End of the Nineteenth Century* (Honolulu: University of Hawai'i Press, 1996), 278–312.

depictions of late nineteenth-century New Zealand—in both *Brighter Britain!* and *The Doom of the Great City*—may reflect Macaulay's influential account of "some traveller from New Zealand" who "shall, in the midst of a vast solitude, take his stand on a broken arch of London Bridge to sketch the ruin of St. Paul's."[19] Nikki Hessell reads this account from an Indigenous studies perspective, emphasizing that in 1840 "New Zealander" referred specifically "to Māori as the sovereign peoples of Aotearoa." She suggests how the image bridges literary discourses and British diplomatic objectives as an intentional and

19. Thomas Macaulay, "Review, *The Ecclesiastical and Political History of the Popes of Rome, during the Sixteenth and Seventeenth Centuries,* by Leopold Ranke," (1840) in *Critical and Historical Essays, Contributed to the Edinburgh Review in Three Volumes* (London: Longman, Brown, Green, and Longmans, 1848), 3:209. David Skilton indicates that "[t]he prediction of the future ruin of London was anticipated by Walpole, Goldsmith, Barbauld, Shelley and others, while the New Zealander himself ultimately derived from a comment in Gibbon's *Decline and Fall* on the Picts who were reported once to have roamed Strathclyde" (3). Belich writes explicitly that "Macaulay's New Zealander . . . had absolutely nothing to do with New Zealand, which was mentioned as one might cite Timbuktu, or Furthest Tartary or the Back of Beyond." He adds that this image of the "antipodean New Zealand" was "a minor convention in British culture" and "related to the Green and Noble Savage" (297–98). For additional discussion of the genealogy of this popular itinerant Māori character, see Skilton, "Contemplating the Ruins of London: Macaulay's New Zealander and Others," *Literary London: Interdisciplinary Studies in the Representation of London* 2, no.1 (March 2004): 1–15; Hunter Dukes, "'When London Is in Ruins': Gustave Doré's *The New Zealander*," *Public Domain Review*, October 26, 2021, and Chris Elliott, "The Needle and the New Zealander: Cleopatra's Needle as Memento Mori for Empire," *Aegyptiaca: Journal of the History of Reception of Ancient Egypt* 5 (2020): 434–45.

functional representation.[20] Macaulay's notion of a mysterious, itinerant figure from New Zealand became so popular that *Punch* satirically banned "Macaulay's New Zealander," proclaiming, "He can no longer be suffered to impede the traffic over London Bridge. Much wanted at the present time in his own country. May return when London is in ruins."[21] Mr. Punch's comments on the recurrent cultural representation of Macaulay's wandering, postapocalyptic New Zealander highlight an absence: the Māori figure has been displaced, deprived of his individuality, and made into a hackneyed trope by British thinkers to herald the future desolation of London and signify the emptiness and availability of colonial lands.[22] Hunter Dukes suggests that Macaulay's concept "predicts, in a sense, the anxieties of 'reverse colonization' that fester in the British imagination across the late-nineteenth and twentieth centuries" and mentions *The Doom of the Great City* as a text "most indebted to Macaulay's idea." Dukes may be right that Hay

20. Nikki Hessell, *Sensitive Negotiations: Indigenous Diplomacy and British Romantic Poetry* (Albany: SUNY Press, 2021), 197–98. "Aotearoa" is the contemporary Māori-language name for New Zealand. For more on the Treaty of Waitangi, see note 25.

21. "A Proclamation," *Punch* 48, no. 7 (January 1865): 9.

22. Blanchard Jerrold made explicit reference to Macaulay's concept in *London: A Pilgrimage* (1872), in which he collaborated with the French artist and printmaker Gustave Doré to detail mundane events and experiences of Victorian London. Doré's "The New Zealander" is the final plate of the collection, and Jerrold describes the character as a "tourist." Gustave Doré and Blanchard Jerrold, *London: A Pilgrimage* (1872; New York: Benjamin Gloom, 1968), 190.

borrows from Macaulay to envision his novella's urban catastrophe and fictionalize cultural fears about invasions or loss, but this persistent image of a traveling Māori man also serves to reify the systematic removal of Indigenous peoples from their lands and homes, resulting in a cultural understanding of New Zealand as vacant.

Writers like Butler, Grey, and Hay contribute to this reification by perpetuating cultural perceptions of New Zealand as empty, savage, or primed for settlement. In his 1885 preface to *Polynesian Mythology, and Ancient Traditional History of the New Zealand Race*, Grey addresses his early challenges as colonial governor and notes that he "could neither successfully govern, nor hope to conciliate, a numerous and turbulent people, with whose language, manners, costumes, religion, and modes of thought I was quite unacquainted."[23] He commits himself to learning "the ancient language of the country, to collect its traditional poems and legends, to induce their priests to impart to me their mythology, and to study their proverbs."[24] Grey was one of the most vital British statesmen in the colonization process of New Zealand, especially during the New Zealand Wars of the mid-nineteenth century, in which Māori tribes lost vast lands because of manipulative translations of the 1840

23. Sir George Grey, *Polynesian Mythology, and Ancient Traditional History of the New Zealand Race, As Furnished by Their Priests and Chiefs* (London: John Murray, Albemarle Street, 1855), iii.
24. Grey, *Polynesian Mythology*, viii.

Treaty of Waitangi.[25] He presents his supposed cultural knowledge of New Zealand as integral to benevolent diplomatic
skills: "to win their confidence and regard . . . and, even if I
could not assist them, to give them a kind reply, couched in
such terms as should leave no doubt on their minds that I
clearly understood and felt for them, and was really well disposed towards them."[26] He casts the Māori as easily affected
people who appear amenable to foreigners occupying their
lands and altering their futures; Tuhiwai Smith adds that Grey,
like other early European explorers, "had a deep sympathy
towards Māori people as an ideal while being hostile towards
those Māori who fell short of this construct."[27] Hay would
almost certainly have read Grey's influential work, and he may
very well have been familiar with Butler's treatments in *A First
Year in Canterbury Settlement* (1863) and *Erewhon; or Over the
Range* (1872). Butler memorably depicts the South Island of
New Zealand (Te Waipounamu) as fertile, beautiful, but unde-
rutilized by its Indigenous residents: "The colony was one

25. The New Zealand government has reproduced the English and Māori
translations of the 1840 Treaty of Waitangi, and its reproduction points to
meaningful differences between the texts. Ministry for Culture and Heritage, "Read the Treaty," available at New Zealand History, http://nzhistory
.govt.nz/politics/treaty/read-the-treaty/english-text, last modified June 20,
2020. For an extensive discussion of the manipulative techniques used by
Great Britain to acquire consent from Māori leaders, see Belich, *Making
Peoples*, 180–211.
26. Grey, *Polynesian Mythology*, iv.
27. Tuhiwai Smith, *Decolonizing Methodologies*, 86.

which had not been opened up even to the most adventurous settlers for more than eight or nine years, having been previously uninhabited, save by a few tribes of savages, who frequented the seaboard."[28] He erases the island's history prior to colonization by describing it as "uninhabited," even as he acknowledges an existing tribal population in the same sentence. Butler leverages this assessment to explain the facile exploitation of the land: "[O]nce Europeans set foot upon this territory they were not slow to take advantage of its capabilities. Sheep and cattle were introduced, and bred with extreme rapidity; men took up their 50,000 or 100,000 acres of country, going inland one behind the other, till in a few years there was not an acre between the sea and the front ranges which was not taken up."[29] He describes New Zealand as a consummate site for British colonization: it is lush, open, and populated with few Indigenous occupants to disrupt new settlements.

Throughout *Brighter Britain!*, Hay celebrates the great achievements of British colonial ventures in New Zealand and borrows from thinkers like Macaulay, Grey, and Butler to showcase the promise of the land that his narrator in *The Doom of the Great City* enjoys. He writes in detail about his rural farmstead: "The grass on our clearings is rich and abundant, and, owing to the nature of the soil, keeps fresh and green all through the dry season, when other districts are crying out

28. Samuel Butler, *Erewhon; or Over the Range* (London: Trübner, 60 Paternoster Row, 1872), 2.
29. Butler, *Erewhon*, 3.

against the drought."[30] New Zealand, according to Hay, offers British emigrants the chance to become long-term inhabitants, just twenty years after the notorious land grabs of the New Zealand Settlements Act of 1863.[31] He extols the ends of colonialism, invites residents of dirty, overcrowded English cities to maximize the yields of supposedly available terrain, and models the enjoyment of New Zealand's grandeur as their own ostensibly well-deserved right: "What we have is our own. We have had years of incessant toil, the hardest possible work, with plenty of food, but little comfort and no holidays to speak of. Two or three years more of it, and then we shall be in a condition to really enjoy the prosperity we have laboured for."[32] His narrative encourages British men and women to travel to New Zealand, adhere to his example as a settler-colonist, and earn their rewards, including the license to own and repopulate the islands like the narrator of *The Doom of the Great City*.[33]

---

30. Hay, *Brighter Britain!* 1:197.
31. The New Zealand Settlements Act of 1863 allowed for the confiscation of the land following a series of proclamations from Governor Grey ordering Indigenous peoples "to take oaths of allegiance and give up arms" following a rebellion against the Queen. See Grey's proclamations cited in Simon Dench, "Representing the Waikato: Photography and Colonisation," *Journal of New Zealand Literature* 29 (2011): 74 and New Zealand Settlements Act, Vict. Reginæ, no. 8 (1863), available through the New Zealand Legal Information Institute at http://www.nzlii.org/nz/legis/hist_act/nzsa186327v1863n8377/.
32. Hay, *Brighter Britain!* 1:198.
33. For a discussion of the lure of New Zealand to British emigrants, see Belich, *Making Peoples*, 376–410.

British emigration to New Zealand in the nineteenth century did not take place in the wake of an urban apocalypse, but it did coincide with evolving cultural conceptions of non-Western peoples and lands that, even today, continue to legitimize ongoing colonialism. In *Decolonizing Methodologies*, Tuhiwai Smith incisively announces:

> It galls us that Western researchers and intellectuals can assume to know all that it is possible to know of us, on the basis of their brief encounters with some of us. It appalls us that the West can desire, extract and claim ownership of our ways of knowing, our imagery, the things we create and produce, and then simultaneously reject the people who created and developed those ideas and seek to deny them further opportunities to be creators of their own culture and own nations.[34]

Tuhiwai Smith's indictment of short-sighted "Western researchers and intellectuals" affirms the continuities between Victorian practices of reproducing limited and strategic ideas about New Zealand and present-day appropriations of Indigenous cultures under the guise of "research." Victorian thinkers deployed these notions to manufacture a cultural discourse on New Zealand that justifies imperialism and erases Indigenous Māori peoples.[35] Hay's *The Doom of the Great City* does not

34. Tuhiwai Smith, *Decolonizing Methodologies*, 1.
35. Sarah Comyn and Porscha Fermanis's edited collection, *Worlding the South: Nineteenth-Century Literary Culture and the Southern Settler*

provide an authentic story *about* New Zealand. Rather, it is a fictional fabrication that renders Māori land as a colonizer's paradise—cultivating a narrative that, even today, enables some to defend the seizure and settlement of others' lands as justifiable solutions to impending anthropogenic disasters.[36]

THE LONDON FOG, CLIMATE DANGER, AND CULTURAL APATHY

Hay's portrait of London's moral decay and ecological destruction revolves around the deadly fog, which serves as a distinctive feature of the capital's modern economy and the nation's wide-ranging imperial networks. As Victorian society transitioned from an agrarian society to an industrial empire, it

---

Colonies (Manchester: Manchester University Press, 2021), is an example of scholarship that attempts to redress this long-standing imperial practice. In their introduction, Comyn and Fermanis note that "a recurring argument in many of our chapters is that the south as we know it today was to a large extent produced at the intersection of nineteenth-century literary, cartographic, political, legal, and economic discourses rather than being a predefined spatial, ontological, and/or conceptual category" (5).

36. The intersections of environmentalism, colonization, and race ideology that continue into the twentieth-century and present day are explored at greater depth through the concept of "Ecofascism." For more on this, see Kristy Campion, "Defining Ecofascism: Historical Foundations and Contemporary Interpretations in the Extreme Right," *Terrorism and Political Violence* 35, no. 4 (2023): 926–44; Janet Biehl and Peter Staudenmaier, *Ecofascism: Lessons from the German Experience* (Edinburgh: AK Press, 1995); and Jerry Harris, "Our Future: Ecosocialism or Ecofascism," *International Journal of Interdisciplinary Global Studies* 17, no. 2 (2022): 35–47.

depleted the natural resources of its homeland and colonies. Nineteenth-century Britain relied upon fossil fuels (primarily coal) to maximize the power of Watt's steam engine, profit from the labor potential of its booming population, and advance systems of global commercialism that spurred major climatic events.[37] These processes, according to Miller, required Britain to transition "away from an organic economy" into "the world's first extraction-based economy." She explains how this system was marked by "finitude and non-reproducibility" because "extractive industry can never benefit from regeneration or replenishment of its product but only move on to a new vein or a new site."[38] Hay's narrator references this extractive practice when he ties London's growth to "the huge and reckless consumption of coal carried on over the wide-extending city, the smoke from which, not being re-consumed or filtered off in any way, was caught up and retained by the vapour-laden air" (93). His description may presage London's fictional end, and Miller helps us theorize the planetary implications of ecological catastrophes that result from extractive economics: unending demands for new mining sites, resources to exhaust, and

---

37. For a further discussion of this development, see Elizabeth Carolyn Miller, *Extraction Ecologies and the Literature of the Long Exhaustion* (Princeton: Princeton University Press, 2021), 6–15; Jesse Oak Taylor, *The Sky of Our Manufacture: The London Fog in British Fiction from Dickens to Woolf* (Charlottesville: University of Virginia Press, 2016), 1–15; and Christine L. Corton, *London Fog: The Biography* (Cambridge, MA: Belknap Press of Harvard University Press, 2015), 1–28.
38. Miller, *Extraction Ecologies*, 6, 7, 8.

ultimately lands to inhabit as cities become polluted, overpopulated, and vulnerable. In *The Sky of Our Manufacture*, Taylor concludes that the "rail networks and steamships [that] connected the country, the city, and the world" helped "London [become] the capital of the first human society to pass into industrial modernity–only to discover that modernity is haunted, and that its ghost leaves carbon footprints."[39] By the middle of the nineteenth century, London served as the metropole of interconnected domestic and colonial systems. *The Doom of the Great City* documents the perils of the city's tremendous development, including specific climatic effects—most notably, of course, the toxic fog.

Hay treats the capital's fog as a weather condition that somehow derives from the unnatural behavior of London's residents *and* the city's industrial production. This convoluted explanation reflects both evolving nineteenth-century popular understandings and the vast confusion that permeates the story. After maligning the city's inhabitants for their excesses, the narrator certifies that "[t]he fog was the most disagreeable and dangerous of all the climatic sufferings that Londoners had to bear"; he soon adds that "[t]he late years of incessant rain and cold had proved conducive to the prevalence of fogs" (93, 94). *The Doom of the Great City* denotes markers of localized climate change, and the residents of this fictional London recognize these signs. We learn that they "were well accustomed" to the fogs and viewed them as "a regular institution, not caring to

39. Taylor, *Sky of Our Manufacture*, 4.

investigate their cause with a view to some means of mitigating them" (93). They accept the fog as a facet of their day-to-day lives, and as Christine L. Corton delineates, Hay's dramatic treatment contributes to an evolving public perception of the fog. She writes, the "true London fog, thick, yellow, and all-encompassing, was born in the 1840s" as part of "the early stages of the industrial revolution in the capital."[40] Numerous mid-nineteenth-century popular writers, most prominently Dickens, represented the city's fog as a literary trope, often as an indicator of mystery or ambiguity, while later in the century, *Punch* published a series of ominous cartoons depicting the figures of King Coal and the Fog Demon. These images, as Taylor argues, were "explicit in linking the smoke of Old King Coal to the high levels of carbonic acid and other chemicals in the fog . . . and to a host of health problems: asthma, bronchitis, pneumonia, pleurisy, and ultimately the death promised in the skulled countenance of the demon itself."[41] The visualizations of King Coal and the Fog Demon correspond with what Corton identifies as a pronounced shift in the cultural discourse on London's fog "in the 1880s, when its repeated visitations during the winter months caused widespread social anxiety . . . and inspired many writers to treat it as a looming presence, alive and malignant."[42] Hay is one of several later

---

40. Corton, *London Fog*, 1.

41. Taylor, *Sky of Our Manufacture*, 103–4. See Taylor's discussion of this *Punch* series in the same work, 97–104.

42. Corton, *London Fog*, 1.

Victorian figures who made explicit the menace of London fogs, such as Francis Albert Rollo Russell, who authored the influential pamphlet, *London Fogs* (1880) and Robert Barr, who published the alarming short story "The Doom of London" (1892).[43] And yet, the people of Hay's novella initially treat the event of February 2, 1882, as a mundane occurrence. Many continue daily activities despite the dark fog and the narrator even reflects, after the fact, "How wonderful it seems to me, looking back upon these events, that the warning never came until too late to be of service." The fog is at once deadly, predictable, and strangely comforting, and the people of London do not deem it an imminent "cause for alarm" until the warning is "too late to be of service" (102). It is immense, yet ordinary; it signals a climatic exigency, and it is also familiar.

Hay's treatments of people's hesitant, slow, and indecisive responses to the fog accentuate the unexpectedness of the calamity, even though he mentions new weather patterns that

43. Ailise Bulfin argues Hay likely drew on Russell's meteorological work, which "accords with Hay's conclusion that large-scale urban settlements were gravely deleterious to human health and unsustainable in their current practices." Ailise Bulfin, "The Natural Catastrophe in Late Victorian Popular Fiction: 'How Will the World End?'" *Critical Survey* 27, no. 2 (2015): 86. Numerous scholars have discussed the similarities between the tales of Barr and Hay, both of which include fantastic measures to illustrate the menace of London's fog. See also Edward Fawcett's *Hartmann the Anarchist; or, The Doom of the Great City* (London: Edward Arnold, 1893). See also Bill Luckin, "'The Heart and Home of Horror': The Great London Fogs of the Late Nineteenth Century," *Social History* 28, no. 1 (January 2003): 31–48.

augur a possible climate emergency. The narrator introduces an
unsettling paradox when he portrays the popular dismissal of
the fog's threat and immediately confirms this threat—a haunting trend in discourses of anthropogenically induced climate
change that perpetuates apathy, misinformation, and inaction.
He acknowledges "how strangely fixed in the London mind
was the notion that their fog was always to be, what it always
had been, innocuous to the generality of people—an idea which
had served to prevent any steps being taken in the direction of
rendering it really so." He then imagines the fog as a clear and
present danger to the city: "a direct destroyer" (105).[44] The
latter portions of the story are littered with startling images of
unanticipated tragedies: scenes of mass chaos, countless dead
who neglected warnings, and people who abruptly expire while
trying to escape the city. While visiting a tavern, for example,
the narrator observes "all the dreadful confusion of sudden
death, in all the hideous contortion of paralyzed panic . . . the
mortal remains of those who had been sitting joyously supping,
when the hour of doom had struck" (122). He later visits a

---

44. Earlier in the story, while discussing the fog with Mr. and Wilton Forrester, the narrator also expresses a viewpoint that anticipates the logic
advanced by many critics or deniers of global warming. He writes, "[T]he
present fog had lasted since Christmas, and was not so thick to-day as it had
been sometimes previously. My argument therefore was, that as the fogs had
not before been found directly hostile to life, it was to be presumed they
were not so now, since no distinctly new element had been imported into
them" (26). Later, we learn of a report that uses similar logic to absolve the
fog from any responsibility for five hundred deaths: "[T]his *could not* have
been the true reason, *because it was contrary to all previous experience*" (33).

London theater and distinguishes "soft and delicate women . . .
still emanating the perfume and rich odours of the toilette"
(123). Our chronicler highlights the fog's extraordinary lethal-
ity by detailing numerous examples of "sudden death," including corpses "entwined together in a twisted, contorted heap,
that made me fancy I could even behold the writhing . . . the
spasm and terror of sudden death" (114). The atmospheric
condition to which people of the capital had grown accustomed becomes an indiscriminate killer that precipitously deci-
mates its population. In her 2018 introduction to a landmark
volume of *Victorian Studies*, Miller writes, "[W]hile it would be
too simplistic to say that Victorian England is answerable for
the [contemporary] climate crisis, it would also be an error to
discount its unique historical role in cultivating the fossil fuel
economy and the resulting surge in greenhouse gas emissions."[45]
She invites us to share in "a project [that] is not one of mere
presentism, nor even [of] strategic presentism, but rather of
acknowledging the dialectical relationship between past and
present: the past makes the present, but the present continually
prompts us to reinterpret significant events, words, and ideas of
the past, thus changing our sense of how, exactly, the past has
created the present."[46] Hay's narrative is a vital text for such a
project that helps us consider the historical, enduring, and
potentially immediate effects of human-induced climate

45. Elizabeth Carolyn Miller, "Climate Change and Victorian Studies:
Introduction," *Victorian Studies* 60, no. 4 (2018): 538–39.
46. Miller, "Climate Change and Victorian Studies," 540.

change, including the public health challenges of modern urban living.

THE FOG, SCIENTIFIC AUTHORITY, AND PUBLIC HEALTH MISINFORMATION

The Doom of the Great City employs medical terminology in an attempt to define the fog's distressing health effects. During the narrator's visit with the Forresters, he participates in a dialogue that reveals Hay's efforts to establish scientific authority and augments the underlying mystery surrounding the astonishing weather event. The elder Mr. Forrester boldly asserts, for example, that "there was clear evidence that the fog injured health, even to the point of proving very quickly fatal to old people, and to those who were suffering from chest complaints or pulmonary weakness of any kind." He accepts that the fog is generally hazardous, cites "statistics of the death-rate [that] showed this to be so beyond dispute," but still hesitates to believe the deadly report shared by the narrator "because it really seemed too much in the nature of a fable" (98–99). Mr. Forrester and others routinely quote empirical data and then often immediately question or reject the impacts of such findings; the elder gentleman can certainly fathom such dangers in "some distant period of the future," but he struggles to imagine "their actual occurrence now" (99). Science, in short, is a powerful tool for debating the mysteries of the fog, but it is not necessarily empowered or entrusted to help us understand the perils of present weather conditions. Hay was quite familiar with the methods, assumptions, and limitations of scientific inquiry; he engaged investigative processes in his later work on mycology, including his *Elementary Text-Book of British Fungi* (1887), and in his 1888 novel, *Blood: A Tragic Tale*, discusses diseases and the practice of transfusion. He skillfully incorporates scientific discourses within his writings, but in his tale of urban apocalypse, he also displays a reluctance to uphold the supposed credibility of science or adhere to its conclusions.

In *The Doom of the Great City*, he specifically considers new, potentially unsettling developments in Victorian medicine, including novel ideas about epidemiology. Brett Beasley addresses Hay's investment in nineteenth-century science and notes how he "goes so far as to include footnotes referencing actual medical authorities."[47] The text, according to Beasley, captures "a time in which science and the emerging discipline of public health were in a state of flux," as "long-held views about the causes and consequences of diseases were being eroded by new findings, especially the germ theory of disease."[48] The narrator's conversation with the Forresters about the fog reflects these cultural uncertainties associated with such nascent ideas. The elder Mr. Forrester proposes that the London air

47. Brett Beasley, "Bad Air: Pollution, Sin, and Science Fiction in William Delisle Hay's *The Doom of the Great City,*" *Public Domain Review* (September 30, 2015): 7.
48. Beasley, "Bad Air," 10. For additional discussion of Hay's treatment of medicine and science, see ibid. 7–12 and Bulfin, "Natural Catastrophe in Late Victorian Popular Fiction," 82–86.

experienced "extraordinary chemical changes . . . by which carbonic oxide would be formed in prodigious quantity" (100). He speculatively links the public health crisis to the possibility of "an electrified condition" in the sky, but the medical practitioner Dr. Wilton Forrester promptly disputes his father's hypothesis and announces, "No; I see only one way in which the fog is likely to act as a life-destroying agent . . . as a rapid and immediate extinguisher of vitality the cause must be bronchial spasm." While he briefly broaches the possibility of the fog transmitting an epidemic, he quickly clarifies, "[E]ach inspiration draws into the lungs a quantity of gritty particles . . . mechanically choking the passages; hence follows spasm of the bronchi, spasm of the glottis" (101). Dr. Forrester methodically diagnoses the symptoms of the deadly fog and designates its operations within the human body, but he hopelessly concludes, "There would not be the chance of a recovery. . . . We only know that [the fogs] have tended to become 'worse,' as we express it, of late years" (101–102). He has few answers, but he vocalizes the threats of predictable, increasingly escalating health hazards.[49]

49. Early in the story, at the close of his winding jeremiad, the narrator may also presage imminent localized change, revolution, or even destruction when he writes, "Already Republicanism was whispered in the public-houses, and Socialism was not unknown in London, though these were chiefly of exotic growth; while there were men of a different type—men who dared to think for themselves, who looked for the coming of some social cataclysm, and who were heard to compare the 'Great City' to those Cities of the Plain that the old Biblical legend tells of as being destroyed by fire from heaven" (90–91).

In a brief story replete with massive death and mounting panic, Hay's characters take time to deliberate the health risks of the fog but devote little energy to preventing or reducing these risks—a feature of the story that anticipates our ongoing inability to redress the dire conditions of the Anthropocene. Dr. Forrester and his father even present the threat of the fog as an established fact. The latter claims it was "evident . . . that the fogs were becoming aggravated every year, and the injury they did was increasing in due proportion;" the former points to a patient "a couple of winters ago," a case study from the fog of 1880 in which "[t]he cause of death was evident from the state of the lungs and air-passages, which were highly congested" (98–99, 100). Both men acknowledge existing information about the fog, and yet, Dr. Forrester, the medical authority in the novella, offers dispiriting closing remarks: "The more I study these things in my mind the gloomier become my forebodings. . . . Scientists have indeed made suggestions, but no steps have as yet been taken to determine their practical utility" (102). His words echo the narrator's earlier assessment of the public's attitude toward the fog: "[N]o one seemed to think the 'institution' other than a huge joke, and not a serious evil to be earnestly combated by science" (94). The novella documents the recognized perils of anthropogenic climate change to humans and the environment as well as the deferral of "suggestions" to address these perils, creating perpetual future local and global hazards. In Hay's work, the fog is a defining feature of the capital and its dissolute population, a toxic killer, and the result of modern industrialization, urbanization, extractivism, and settler colonialism. It also serves as a manifestation of Londoners' estranged relationship with nature; while the fog is part of the city's ecology, it is the artificial product of human activity, and this artifice impedes the discovery of pragmatic policy solutions. The dialogue between the Forresters and our storyteller reminds us of ongoing discussions on global warming, public health, or world hunger, in which we find ourselves "too late" to remedy an awful consequence that "we have long known to be an intolerable nuisance, and [which] seems about to become a very grave evil" (102). The danger of the fog is not in doubt, but Hay illustrates how people's indifference and indulgent behavior leaves the capital and its growing population vulnerable to more confusion, devastation, and terror.

THE CHAOS, CONFUSION, AND TERRORS OF LONDON'S SUBURBANIZATION

The Doom of the Great City reflects London's remarkable nineteenth-century expansion that historians have thoroughly discussed.[50] This urbanization, of course, coincided with Britain's industrialization and the height of its global imperial network; it also involved a corresponding process of suburbanization. Sarah Bilston reports that "Britain became an urban nation" in

---

50. Interestingly, even Hay points to such extensive discussions when he notes that "descriptions of London are plentiful, and every school-boy is familiar with them, while much also has been written about its inhabitants at that period" (79).

the 1800s, "meaning that more people lived in cities than in the countryside by 1851." She specifies that "the population of London alone swelled from under one million in 1800 to four and a half million in 1900."[51] In *Greater London: The Story of the Suburbs*, Nick Barratt examines the concurrent development of suburbs surrounding the British capital. He explains how "there were few restrictions to curb urban sprawl" and notes that "between 1831 and 1851 the overall number of London residents jumped from 1.9 million to 2.65 million."[52] Hay references this phenomenon when his narrator bemoans that "[f]or miles and miles around us on every side were streets and squares and endless ranks of houses, ever extending outwards, and absorbing suburb after suburb beneath stone and brick" (78). This massive population boom necessitated significant adjustments to the city's infrastructure, including additional housing, systems of mass transportation, and modernized public utilities. Victorian social critics scrutinized the failures and shortcomings of many such reforms and advancements, and Barratt maintains that "the spread of suburban rail networks, linking what had been satellite towns and villages to metropolitan London, encouraged new building and development on an awe-inspiring scale."[53] He cites statistical records that reveal how the population increased to 6.5 million by 1900

51. Sarah Bilston, *The Promise of the Suburbs: A Victorian History in Literature and Culture* (New Haven: Yale University Press, 2019), 3.
52. Nick Barratt, *Greater London: The Story of the Suburbs* (London: Random House Books, 2012), 177.
53. Barratt, *Greater London*, 192.

and concludes that while "some population expansion occurred close to the centre—notably in Southwark and Tower Hamlets . . . it was really the outer suburbs that made the greatest contribution."[54] Hay's narrator makes numerous allusions to London's rapid growth: the masses' dissolute conduct, crowded trains and stations, and haunting sketches of innumerable dead throughout the capital. He also offers compelling images of suburban life that augment our understandings of Victorian urbanization and the chaos engendered by the fog.

Hay devotes meaningful attention to descriptions of the suburbs, and they feature prominently in the structure of the novella's plot. Early in the story, we learn of the protagonist's family's habit of "occasionally recreating ourselves with a trip to the suburbs" (77). Hay initially associates the suburbs with both leisure and separation; they are a space removed from the crowds, dirt, and debased behavior of London, designated for enjoyable times with relatives and friends. Our storyteller and his family plan a trip to Dulwich to celebrate his birthday with the Forresters, but the fog prevents his mother and sister from accompanying him. He still goes, and this journey creates a physical division between himself and the epicenter of the ecological disaster, where his relations and the other doomed residents of the capital become trapped.[55] Throughout his

---

54. Barratt, *Greater London*, 193.
55. The narrator's willingness to leave his mother and sister behind is striking and informs the emphasis on family in the opening frame story. Later in the story, he addresses his audience directly and states, "[F]or you know, my grandchildren, that those two darling women were all the ties I then had in

travels (to and from the suburbs), the narrator identifies specific locations around the perimeter of the capital that mark this division. For example, he draws particular attention to the "dense brown fog-bank, which lay along the line of the Surrey hills, completely shutting out all view beyond" and functioning as a barrier of sorts, disconnecting satellite communities from the urban center (103). At the Champion Hill railway station, he relates how the fog impedes transport and communication between the city and the suburbs, effectively widening the gap between these spaces. He observes that a "large but awestricken crowd was gathered" and recounts, "All traffic into and out of London was indeed suspended, or rather, had never commenced. . . . no response had been received to signals or telegrams" (107). The narrator and others in the suburbs are cut off from the people and events of the capital; they wait, lacking information and access—the same access that had previously facilitated abundant suburbanization. These scenes, moreover, illustrate the fog's technological, economic, and psychological impact upon suburbanites' relationships to the city of London. Hay describes "[c]rowds of men who lived in the suburbs and were employed in the City by day," and as people become more anxious about the dearth of updates from London, their uncertainty soon develops into "a dreadful panic" that Hay invites us to consider as distinctly suburban (107).

---

the world; on them my whole affections were centred; they were the sum and substance of my life" (118).

Confusions of various kinds infuse the novella as people are trapped "in a fog," and while Hay initially attributes this uncertainty to rumors and unverified reports, he also dramatizes how such speculations prompt suburban scenes of chaos and ultimately terror. On the train to the suburbs, the narrator remembers, "[I]t was too murky within the carriage . . . for the passengers to distinguish one another very clearly." But despite such visual impairment, he reports how "conversation was carried on, perhaps all the more volubly on that account" (95). Sixty years following the event, he recites overheard dialogues, directly quoting one agitated man who himself transmits secondhand news: "Some said there was hundreds dead, and others said it was not above a dozen altogether. I don't know, nobody seemed to know, the rights of it; they couldn't, you see, the fog was still so dense" (96). While our aged storyteller had previously assured his grandchildren that he would only dictate his direct observations, he now discloses a passenger's gossip-laden testimony, which fuels increasing fears about the fog as well as people's pervasive ignorance. The following morning, as the narrator awakes seemingly secure in the safety of the suburbs, "neither the post nor the papers made their appearance" (103). Later that day, the evening paper announces that "over five hundred lives were certainly lost, but that, owing to the dense fog in the locality . . . the exact total could not yet be known" (105). Hay's language again emphasizes the uncertainties surrounding the fog, its threat, and its movements. Even as the narrator and other characters glean ostensible data, they heighten a mystery, underscoring how much "could not yet be known."

This lack of clarity impedes efforts to assess the fog and mitigate its risks, resulting in suburban chaos that soon devolves into terror. At Lordship Lane, a prominent commercial area of East Dulwich, "[p]eople were rushing wildly to and fro . . . on the pavement, inside and outside of the public-houses and the shops" (106). As people come to terms with this iteration of the fog, their confusion develops into "panic, terror, fear," and they express these emotions in public sites of consumerism (106). The narrator recalls how this rising terror disrupts suburban routines, comforts, and social relations:

> Instead of the accustomed noise, bustle, and brisk hurry, white-faced groups consulted together in whispering tones; and many, utterly demoralized by excess of terror, had gone home to carry off their families to some place of greater safety. All round the "Great City" lay a wide belt of suburban districts, and these were now—so it seemed—given up to confusion, peopled with panic, invaded with dismay. (107–108)

The expansive "white-faced" suburban population dismisses its familiar daily activities and succumbs to "confusion." Residents have lost their composure—composure, in part, fashioned by the reputed safety of their distanced communities. Bilston affirms that the London suburbs offered great promise, especially for people moving from the countryside toward the city; "to choose a suburban home was to move *toward* opportunity."[56] This

---

56. Bilston, *Promise of the Suburbs*, 5.

suburban promise or potential, however, has also been tied to what Bilston identifies as the "dull, ridiculous, monstrous, or all three," and she adds that "the image of the dull, silly, and tasteless suburb reflects and embodies anxiety about the middle class and its efforts to establish and understand itself in the nineteenth and early twentieth centuries."[57] As more reports about the deadly fog filter into the suburbs, inhabitants manifest their anxieties as terror, rather than the "jokes" and "amusing anecdotes" that the Forrester daughters exchanged just one day prior, during the "pleasant evening that followed dinner" (97–98).[58] Hay's novella may anticipate future representations of middle-class isolation, insecurity, and boredom in twenty-first-century films like *Insidious*, *Get Out!*, and *It Follows*, as we see the horrors that lie beneath the calm veneer of suburban life. When the narrator begins his awful journey back toward London, he reports how "the horrid fever of suspense made things seem darker," and "the first consternation spread and deepened until a vast wave of awful, unheard-of terror rushed back from the outskirts of London" (109). The suburbs are no longer a safe site for recreation and opportunity.

As the narrator walks from the suburbs back to the center of London, he witnesses additional examples of mass confusion, paranoia, and horror, including abundant victims of the fog

---

57. Bilston, *Promise of the Suburbs*, 7, 10.
58. Hay again adopts nostalgic rhetoric of domesticity when discussing the Forresters, describing them as "a genial, old-fashioned family, inhabiting a comfortable, old-fashioned house standing in its own walled garden, and looking down upon the trim plastered villas that were springing up all around it" (96).

who tried to escape the danger too late or who continued to believe that such weather was simply part of everyday life.[59] He identifies "the 'Great City' beyond us . . . stupefied, paralysed, to all seeming devoid of life" (109). This distant view of the lifeless capital overwhelms the narrator, who notes his solitude "at an hour—it was now approaching noon—when it was usually busiest" (109). During his journey, he reflects upon London's lifelessness and acknowledges his growing despair: "I saw no living being, no faces at the shrouded windows, no passers by, no children playing in the gardens or the road" (111). He also alerts readers to specific sites: Camberwell Green, Vauxhall Bridge, Buckingham Palace, St. James's Park, Trafalgar Square, the Strand, Charing Cross. His attention to geographical detail lends authority and order to his memoir as it helps us to map his movement from the southern suburbs, back across the Thames to the center of the city; moreover, his various depictions of Londoners who died during their desperate attempts to

---

59. At various points throughout the final third of the novella, the narrator recollects his separation from his mother and sister and vocalizes his desire to reconnect with them. He initially presents this desire as his motivation for returning to London: "The recollection of my mother and sister came before my mind so strongly that I resolved instantly to make my way to them. I intimated my resolution to the Forresters, my companions. They did not attempt to dissuade me, but the old man wrung my hand and said, 'Come back to us, my lad, if—' and he nodded and turned away. Then I passed on my road into London" (110). As he journeys, the devastation of the fog distracts him, and he forgets about his family. He later reflects, "It was strange that all this while I had not felt any distinct apprehension for my mother and sister. I had not connected them in my mind with the idea of death" (117).

flee the city allows him to determine "that the crisis occurred at different hours in several localities" (113). At Camberwell Green, for example, he "saw three cabs standing on the rank; the horses had fallen and were lying dead between the shafts, while at a little distance an indistinct mass upon the sidewalk was probably the bodies of the drivers" (112). His emphasis on location informs our sense of time and place in the story, as does the ambiguity of his description: the travelers' corpses have quickly transmogrified into "an indistinct mass," embodying the confusion that undergirds the catastrophe. After recording numerous other awful scenes, he admits, "For sixty years I have prayed unceasingly that the hideous memories of that awful day might be blotted from my mind" (114). Despite all the uncertainty, mystery, and ambiguity in the novella, our narrator has not managed to forget such "memories" and instead tells his readers, "I turned in an excess of horror from that grim load of dead. . . . So great was the effect of these horrors upon my mind" (114).[60] His trip back into the heart of London exposes him to the magnitude of the fog's devastation. Still, he not only

---

60. The narrator repeatedly emphasizes his visual authority as a first-hand witness as well as his attempts to forget, limit, or occlude his observations. He also notes, for example, how "the fog, unmerciful before, had mercy to me then; its loathsome mantle shrouded numberless deadly horrors from my view, and veiled a veritable Valley of the Shadow of Death as I passed through it" (114–15). He immediately adds, "I kept my eyes bent upon the ground, and held along the tramway, not daring to look up in case my eyes might again encounter some fearful spectacle. Often I passed by dark objects of whose dismal character I was but too well convinced, though I avoided their inspection" (115).

recalls this terrifying memory but shares it with his abundant progeny who now populate the pristine, distant lands of New Zealand.

THE PLEASURES OF THE APOCALYPSE

Despite the text's depictions of tremendous chaos, death, and terror, the narrator initiates his story by announcing the immense joys of bequeathing his recollections to his progeny. He writes, "It is with feelings of no little pleasure that I . . . sit down to write to you collectively" and discloses pointed motivations: "I am about to give effect to a narrative that has been long desired on your part . . . I feel that if delayed any longer, it may be that I shall pass away without having told it" (71). His language highlights his descendants' long-standing wish to know the details of the distant apocalyptic event and his anxiety about his own looming end—an end that would terminate the legend of his survival. As a narrator, he has particular reasons to tell this apocalyptic tale, and the telling of his tale accomplishes diverse cultural work. In *A Billion Black Anthropocenes or None* (2018), Yusoff acknowledges that "[t]he Anthropocene might seem to offer a dystopic future that laments the end of the world," but she insists that "imperialism and ongoing (settler) colonialisms have been ending worlds for as long as they have been in existence."[61] Hay's story dramatizes how anthropocenic processes contribute to the extermination

61. Yusoff, *A Billion Black Anthropocenes*, xiii.

of late Victorian London while upholding imperialism as a righteous project that contributes to the erasure of Indigenous lands and peoples. The narrator definitively claims that his settler-colonist life in New Zealand stimulates and solidifies his happiness; he relishes "the joys and pleasures of the numerous family with which I have been blessed" (72). In the brief frame story, he yokes together the celebration of his eighty-fourth birthday with the commemoration of the deadly fog and proud declarations of his renewed lineage, merging painful remembrances of the past with pleasures of the present and future. The narrator of *The Doom of the Great City* complies with his grandchildren's repeated requests to impart his memories, and in the process, finds delight in indicting the city's residents, hypothesizing about their deserved demise, and rebuilding a community in distant Indigenous lands.

In a brief story supposedly focused on a fatal climatic event, Hay devotes significant early portions of the narrative to describing London's depravities. In two long-winded paragraphs—each stretching for multiple pages—he traces the corruption of the city to the profuse, injudicious pleasures of its residents and arraigns various peoples and failed institutions. He insists that "[p]leasure-seeking [was] the only employment of the wealthy and governing class," who "elevated it into a 'cult'" and "invented 'aestheticism' as a cloak for higher flights of sin" (82). While he critiques the affluent for their excessive, unnecessary ornamentation, in his description of the lower ranks of society, he faults their "lack of 'refinement'" and insists "it displayed a sense of actual pleasure, where *blasé* and captious disdain ought only to have been manifested" (84). According to the narrator, men of various classes misuse, misperceive, or misrepresent pleasures, but he saves his sharpest reprimands for women, including prostitutes, who "haunted the busier streets . . . where pleasure-seekers congregated" (87). He chastises sex workers for inciting profane desires and directly blames "[l]adies of the wealthy classes" for "their love of dress," which, he claims, negatively affects the loyalties of all women: "women of every rank imitated those above them" and "were prepared to sacrifice fathers, brothers, husbands, relatives and friends, their homes, religion, consciences, virtue and honour—everything, in short—so long as they could flaunt in gorgeous costumes" (88). The inhabitants of Hay's fictional London have pursued extravagant, decadent, dissolute delights that, according to the narrator, hasten, even legitimate their destruction. In the final moments of the story, after traversing "Charing Cross and onwards," he arrives at the Strand, the "part of the town that had been thronged with pleasure-seekers," and provides a gruesome image of death: "[B]odies lay thick as on some battle-field, save that never battle-field was so grimly terrible as this" (119, 124–25). For Hay's narrator, the pleasures of modern London life engender not just death but horrible scenes of militaristic slaughter.

And he finds some semblance of gratification in recording this carnage. Earlier in the story, as he begins to glimpse the extent of the tragedy, he questions his familial audience, "Can you understand now the train of reasoning which led your grandfather to expatiate on all that was vile and wicked in the once-entitled 'Modern Babylon'? Do you not see why I rather recall the evil and forget the good?" (109). He asks his descendants to appreciate, even legitimate the pleasures of his jeremiad, and after detailing the toxic fog and observing vast death, muses, "O London! Surely, great and manifold as were thy wickednesses, thy crimes, thy faults. . . . And I, a lingering survivor of thy slain, oh, pity, that it should have been my task to tell of thy CORRUPTION, to bear witness to thy PUNISHMENT!" As he strolls the streets of the decimated capital, he requests pity for himself, not for the innumerable dead. He fashions himself as a forsaken but heroic figure of sorts, "who dared at that terrible moment to say thy sentence was deserved?" (117). At this point, the narrator cloaks his victim-blaming evaluations of the London public in the rhetoric of reportage, reminding us of his self-acclaimed valor and intensifying his enjoyment as he recounts the story to his healthy, vibrant progeny, who, like himself, are removed from the sins of London and free to savor the delights of empire as settler-colonists on Māori land.

Hay deems the perverted pleasures of London a rationale for the city's annihilation, and his narrator expresses joy as he divulges remembrances of its ruin. His language exposes disturbing qualities of global schadenfreude when he presents the sixtieth anniversary of the devastating fog as "commemorative to the whole world" and invites future readers to share his pleasures: "[M]any besides yourselves would be glad to hear all I have to say about it" (74, 73). The narrator anticipates that others, beyond his grandchildren, will find amusement or happiness or instruction in his account of London's destruction, and he models this experience while conversing with the Forresters on the public health risks of the fog. As he processes horrifying medical diagnoses, he reflects, "I can remember yet the indescribable thrill which passed through me during these conversations" (102). The narrator is exhilarated to learn about the perilous condition of the city's residents; he assumes scientific credentials to diagnose, the moral authority to rebuke, and the privilege to foreground his own satisfaction as a storyteller. Earlier in the story, following his righteous and rambling denunciation of the capital, he restarts his narration by detailing plans for a different birthday event sixty years earlier, announcing that he and his family "anticipated no little pleasure from the excursion, and it was consequently with feelings of delighted expectation" that he awaits the trip (91). The narrator, of course, knows that his comments preface a story of massive death, great turmoil, sincere terror, and settler-colonialism; still, he frames his memories of the urban apocalypse as joyful. This narrative technique reminds us of Yusoff's assertion that "the end of this world has already happened for some subjects, and it is the prerequisite for the possibility of imagining 'living and breathing again' for others."[62] *The Doom of the Great City* suggests that "the end of this world" may very well have "already happened" for late nineteenth-century London. As the narrator introduces his account, he also points to "already" eradicated Indigenous worlds that precipitate his

62. Yusoff, *A Billion Black Anthropocenes*, 12–13.

family's growth, allowing his descendants to live, breathe, and recreate far removed from toxic fogs, mass chaos, and depraved peoples.

Hay provides a more radical example of the pleasures of extinction in *Three Hundred Years Hence; Or, A Voice from Posterity* (1881), a futuristic vision that explicitly confronts what its professorial narrator identifies as the failures of "leaders of men in the latter part of the nineteenth century," who "took no practical hold of the population question."[63] In *The Doom of the Great City*, Hay derides the loss of agrarian lifestyles, the growth of urban areas, and the people who inhabit them; in *Three Hundred Years Hence*, he vastly expands his criticism to denigrate non-white peoples across the world, blaming politicians, economists, and scientists for allowing "the Chinamen . . . to be exceedingly proliferous" and "[c]ertain African tribes . . . to multiply alarmingly."[64] Hay does little to mask the racism of his tale behind the machinery of speculative fiction. He writes bluntly, "[T]he stern logic of facts proclaimed the Negro and the Chinaman below the level of the Caucasian, and incapacitated from advance towards his intellectual standard. To the development of the White Man, the Black Man and the Yellow Man must ever remain inferior."[65] The narrative addresses not local but worldwide problems by

63. William Delisle Hay, *Three Hundred Years Hence; Or, A Voice from Posterity* (London: Newman, 1881), 26.
64. Hay, *Three Hundred Years Hence*, 9.
65. Hay, *Three Hundred Years Hence*, 235–36.

eliminating "inferior" races, and we learn that the ostensible solution was quickly agreed upon by an assembly of white people:

> A low murmur was heard among the people, soon rising into a formidable and definite outcry: "Why do we wait?" said some. "What is to be gained by any longer considering these races as akin to us? Will not our children soon be crying to us for bread? For what do we hesitate? Let us seize upon these countries? Let the inferior give place to the superior! Even religion is on our side, as well as common sense! . . . . So, then, though we may deplore it, though till this last pinch we have put it from us, there is now no other way! Death to the Negro! Annihilation to the Chinaman!'"[66]

In *Three Hundred Years Hence*, the white populations of the planet cite self-preservation—derived from "the logics of the Anthropocene"—to rationalize multiple genocides, and Hay highlights the outcomes of this policy as pleasurable. We learn that "[a]fter the extermination of the Inferior Races there was, at it were, a breathing-space. There were vast tracts of land awaiting occupants, and into which immigrants soon began to flock, changing the aspect of the country as they came, and bringing the advancing civilization of the White Man along with them."[67] Hay envisions a far less congested global community, replete with

66. Hay, *Three Hundred Years Hence*, 237.
67. Hay, *Three Hundred Years Hence*, 259.

more space for "'living and breathing again.'"[68] He declares that as "the advancing civilization of the White Man" became imminent, "[t]he face of Africa changed like a dream; no longer paralysed by the ownership of savage brute and no less savage man . . . blossom[ing] into rich and regular luxuriance of cultivation beneath the White man's tread."[69] He emphasizes the pleasures of hate, state racism, and ethnic cleansing and upholds the "rich and regular luxuriance" of the world created by calculated annihilation—a world in which Black and Brown peoples are absent. In the end, he presents the result of his white supremacist fantasy as a harmonious global community: "not a sect or an order" but "one uniform whole, whose various circles are not divided by absurd and factitious barriers."[70] The deliberate extermination of racialized others produces uniformity, harmony, and a thriving white community, not unlike the extensive lineage celebrated on Māori lands by the settler-colonialist narrator of *The Doom of the Great City*.

Hay publishes *Three Hundred Years Hence* just one year after *The Doom of the Great City*, and the proximity of these texts invites us to consider how each informs the other. *The Doom of the Great City* does not relate the worldwide extermination of non-white peoples, but it may help us imagine the mechanisms, rationales, and for some, pleasures of such present and future genocidal programs within the context of a localized ecological

---

68. Yusoff, *A Billion Black Anthropocenes or None*, 13.
69. Hay, *Three Hundred Years Hence*, 259.
70. Hay, *Three Hundred Years Hence*, 350.

disaster. The novella's depictions of industrial pollution, urban sprawl, and climatic exigency fuel the versatility of Hay's account of anthropocenic crisis. In *The Black Shoals: Offshore Formations of Black and Native Studies*, King tersely asserts that "[f]or the human to continue to evolve as an unfettered form of self-actualizing (and expanding) form of Whiteness, Black and Indigenous people must die or be transformed into lesser forms of humanity–and in some cases, become nonhuman altogether."[71] Hay's narrative documents devastation and regeneration, ruin and renewal, and ultimately renders the continuity of white male supremacy as delightful and the absence of Māori as a fait accompli. King theorizes that "[t]o become or 'ascend' to Whiteness is to enact a self—or self-actualize—in a way that requires the death of others."[72] *The Doom of the Great City* delineates and may even celebrate such requisite death—in London and New Zealand—and the narrator, in turn, manifests his postapocalyptic identity, life, and future family as justified and pleasant. As part of the novella's opening frame, the narrator reflects on the limitations of his own storytelling ability: "[Y]our histories will tell you, better than I could, of preceding events, and more particularly of those great changes which followed and partly resulted from the stupendous accident" (74). Hay's tale identifies many of the hazards, ills, and "great changes" of modernity: imperialism, extractivism, (sub)urbanization, extreme weather events, toxic ecosystems, and

71. Tiffany Lethabo King, *The Black Shoals: Offshore Formations of Black and Native Studies* (Durham, NC: Duke University Press, 2019), 20–21.
72. King, *Black Shoals*, xii.

terrorizing anxiety. He leverages these changes, highlighting some as threats, deemphasizing some as distant, and recasting still others as delights. This technique allows Hay to envision the erasure of Indigenous communities as a benevolent means to the enduring sustainability of white male supremacy.

EDITORIAL NOTE

It was a great editorial challenge to present a text whose author rather openly announces white supremacist sentiments. *The Doom of the Great City* has, up until this point, received scant critical attention, and this volume will enhance Hay's critical status and likely encourage scholars to reinvestigate his writings. We hope these reinvestigations prompt complex, far-reaching discussions, including questions about the merits of reintroducing an author seemingly invested in genocidal and imperialist solutions for local and global problems. Our editorial processes led us to reflect on our methods and their implications. How should we evaluate the cultural function of ecological catastrophe within Hay's fictional world and our own present and future worlds? Can or should we separate the climatic emergency in London from the narrator's settler colonialism in New Zealand? What are the best practices for arranging such literary or cultural works? *The Doom of the Great City* may not express the explicit racism of *Three Hundred Years Hence*, and this creates different difficulties for editing and arranging the novella. The urban apocalypse legitimates and perpetuates white male supremacy as it draws on the techniques of disaster fiction, the subfield of Cli-Fi, and the history of apocalyptic literature. As editors, we have tried to make visible the place of Hay's tale within these different literary traditions, but we have also worked to exhibit its investment in imperialism, racism, and patriarchy. We have not, like the narrator, tried to bury these issues "under sixty years of time"; we have, instead, attempted to emulate the angel of history who views the hatred, suffering, and devastation that mark our past—and perhaps our futures (74).[73] And we have also framed such visions with curated appendices that, we hope, will help teachers, students, and researchers study Hay's narrative alongside vital nineteenth-century conversations that remain relevant. We believe that this editorial technique will allow readers to perceive the story's contributions to a range of scientific, cultural, and literary discourses.

While Hay lived and wrote during a dynamic social and intellectual period, we know strikingly little about the details of his own history. He was born between 1850 and 1853; the date of his death is unknown. While his eclectic works inform our understanding of his personal and professional activities, including travels in New Zealand, time as a Fellow of the Royal Geographical Society, experiments in mycology, and interest in blood transfusions, much of his biography remains unknown. As editors, we have not concerned ourselves with solving or

73. From Walter Benjamin, "On the Concept of History," in *Walter Benjamin: Selected Writings*, vol. 4, *1938–1940*, ed. Howard Eiland and Michael W. Jennings (Cambridge, MA: Belknap Press, 2003), 389–400.

amplifying this mystery; we specifically did not want to risk unintentionally reifying the colonizer-hero fable endorsed by Hay's narrator. We have, instead, organized this edition of *The Doom of the Great City* to accentuate how the text engages key discourses of the Anthropocene: ecological dangers, climatic emergencies, colonialism, (sub)urbanization, industrialism, and the apocalypse. We made deliberate choices in the organization of the appendices of primary materials to deemphasize some canonical, perhaps predictable, nineteenth-century voices commonly associated with these topics. We have not, for example, included selections from Darwin, Galton, Nordau, or Huxley; we have also not included popular late Victorian writers like Wells, Stevenson, or Haggard. We made these decisions not because these thinkers were irrelevant or unimportant to Hay's work but because we felt their writings were often already studied or easily accessible. We have, instead, included a diverse range of excerpts and images that address the local and global implications of the Anthropocene, complicating how we read stories of environmental disaster. Our hope is that this edition will help readers to identify and unsettle the enduring lure of stories of the end.

The narrator of *The Doom of the Great City* explicitly presents his tale as the recollection of a single "event," but the demise of the British capital derives from various interrelated human actions and developments that presage planetary turmoil. In an age of pandemics, climate emergencies, and various forms of political extremism, many find meaning, efficacy, even pleasure in fictional portraits of the end; and these narratives are still used to advance different cultural goals. Hay's succinct account allows for pithy, straightforward, even reductionist interpretations—and even simpler comparisons to contemporary issues. We hope our editorial choices encourage academics and nonacademics alike to explore instead the complexities of Hay's narrative, its many discomforting, even terrifying qualities, and the diverse ways narratives of ecological crises are strategically marshaled toward a variety of ends.

SELECTED BIBLIOGRAPHY AND ADDITIONAL READINGS

HAY'S FICTIONAL WRITINGS

The Doom of the Great City; Being the Narrative of a Survivor, Written A.D. 1942. London: Newman, 1880.

Three Hundred Years Hence; Or, A Voice from Posterity. London: Newman, 1881.

Blood: A Tragic Tale. London: Swan Sonnenschein, 1888.

HAY'S NONFICTION WRITINGS

Brighter Britain! Or, Settler and Maori in Northern New Zealand. 2 vols. London: Richard Bentley and Son, 1882.

An Elementary Text-Book of British Fungi. London: Swan Sonnenschein, Lowrey, 1887.

The Fungus-Hunter's Guide, and Field Memorandum Book.
London: Swan Sonnenschein, Lowrey, 1887.

EDITED AND ARRANGED BY HAY

Wawn, William T. *The South Sea Islanders and the Queensland
Labour Trade: A Record of Voyages and Experiences in the
Western Pacific, from 1875 to 1891*. London: Swan Sonnen-
schein, 1893.

**CRITICISM ON HAY, *DOOM OF THE GREAT CITY*,
AND LATE VICTORIAN DISASTER FICTION**

Beasley, Brett. "Bad Air: Pollution, Sin, and Science Fiction in
William Delisle Hay's *The Doom of the Great City*." *Public
Domain Review*, September 30, 2015, 1–16.

Bradshaw, James Stanford. "The Science Fiction of Robert
Barr." *Science Fiction Studies* 16, no. 2 (July 1989): 201–8.

Bulfin, Ailise. "'The End of Time': M.P. Shiel and the 'Apocalyptic Imaginary.'" In *Victorian Time: Technologies, Stan-
dardizations, Catastrophes*, edited by Trish Ferguson, 153–77.
London: Palgrave Macmillan, 2013.

———. "The Natural Catastrophe in Late Victorian Popular
Fiction: 'How Will the World End?'" *Critical Survey* 27,
no. 2 (2015): 81–101.

Clarke, I. F. "From Space to Time: The Music of Old Earth and
New Time." *Futures* 23, no. 1 (January/February 1991):
59–68.

Elliott, Chris. *Needles from the Nile: Obelisks and the Past as Property*. Liverpool: Liverpool University Press, 2022.

Frost, Mark. "Ecocrisis and Slow Violence: Anthropocene Readings of Late-Victorian Disaster Narratives." In *Victorian Environmental Nightmares*, edited by Laurence W. Mazzeno and Ronald D. Morrison, 243–62. Cham, Switzerland: Palgrave Macmillan, 2019.

Kibbie, Ann Louise. *Transfusion: Blood and Sympathy in the Nineteenth-Century Literary Imagination*. Charlottesville: University of Virginia Press, 2019.

Komsta, Mata Karolina. "A Plunge into Space: Spatial Variations in 19th-Century British Utopias." In *Space in Literature: Method, Genre, Topos*, edited by Urszula Terentowicz-Fotyga, 149–60. Berlin: Peter Lang, 2018.

Luckin, Bill. "'The Heart and Home of Horror': The Great London Fogs of the Late Nineteenth Century." *Social History* 28, no. 1 (January 2003): 31–48.

Rawson, Michael. *The Nature of Tomorrow: A History of the Environmental Future*. New Haven: Yale University Press, 2021.

Reno, Seth T. *Early Anthropocene Literature in Britain, 1750–1884*. Cham, Switzerland: Palgrave Macmillan, 2020.

Suvin, Darko. "Victorian Science Fiction, 1871–85: The Rise of the Alternative History Sub-Genre." *Science Fiction Studies* 10, no. 2 (July 1983): 148–69.

ANTHROPOCENE STUDIES

Crutzen, Paul J., and Eugene F. Stoermer. "The 'Anthropocene.'" In *The Future of Nature: Documents of Global Change*, edited by Libby Robin, Sverker Sörlin and Paul Warde, 483–90. New Haven: Yale University Press, 2013.

Daggett, Cara New. *The Birth of Energy: Fossil Fuels, Thermodynamics, and the Politics of Work*. Durham, NC: Duke University Press, 2019.

Ellis, Erle C. *Anthropocene: A Very Short Introduction*. Oxford: Oxford University Press, 2018.

Fanon, Frantz. *The Wretched of the Earth*. New York: Grove Press, 2004.

Garden, Donald S. *Droughts, Floods, and Cyclones: El Niños That Shaped Our Colonial Past*. North Melbourne: Australian Scholarly Publishing, 2009.

George, Sheldon, and Derek Hook, eds. *Race and Lacan: Racism, Identity, and Psychoanalytic Theory*. London: Routledge, 2021.

Ghosh, Amitav. *The Great Derangement: Climate Change and the Unthinkable*. Chicago: University of Chicago Press, 2016.

Horn, Eva, and Hannes Bergthaller. *The Anthropocene: Key Issues for the Humanities*. London: Routledge, 2020.

Janković, Vladimir. *Reading the Skies: A Cultural History of English Weather, 1650–1820*. Chicago: University of Chicago Press, 2001.

Malm, Andreas. *Fossil Capital: The Rise of Steam Power and the Roots of Global Warming*. London: Verso, 2016.

Markley, Robert. "Literature, Climate, and Time: Between History and Story." In *Climate and Literature*, edited by Adeline Johns-Putra, 15–30. Cambridge, UK: Cambridge University Press, 2019.

McKittrick, Katherine. *Dear Science and Other Stories*. Durham, NC: Duke University Press, 2021.

———. *Demonic Grounds: Black Women and the Cartographies of Struggle*. Minneapolis: University of Minnesota Press, 2006.

Menely, Tobias, and Jesse Oak Taylor, eds. *Anthropocene Reading: Literary History in Geologic Times*. University Park: Penn State University Press, 2017.

Mentz, Steve. *Shipwreck Modernity: Ecologies of Globalization, 1550–1719*. Minneapolis: University of Minnesota Press, 2015.

Merchant, Carolyn. *The Anthropocene and the Humanities: From Climate Change to a New Age of Sustainability*. New Haven: Yale University Press, 2020.

Morton, Timothy. *Dark Ecology: For A Logic of Future Coexistence*. New York: Columbia University Press, 2016.

Trexler, Adam. *Anthropocene Fictions: The Novel in a Time of Climate Change*. Charlottesville: University of Virginia Press, 2015.

Zupančič, Alenka. "The End of Ideology, the Ideology of the End." *South Atlantic Quarterly* 119, no. 4 (2020): 833–44.

SETTLER-COLONIALISM AND THE ANTHROPOCENE

Baishya, Amit R., and Priya Kumar. "Ends of Worlds or the Continuation of the Planet? Postcolonial Theory, the Anthropocene, and the Nonhuman." *Postcolonial Studies* 25, no. 3 (2022): 305–20.

Comyn, Sarah, and Porscha Fermanis, eds. *Worlding the South: Nineteenth-Century Literary Culture and the Southern Settler Colonies*. Manchester: Manchester University Press, 2021.

Davis, Mike. *Late Victorian Holocausts: El Niño Famines and the Making of the Third World*. London: Verso, 2001.

Giuliani, Gaia. *Monsters, Catastrophes, and the Anthropocene: A Postcolonial Critique*. London: Routledge, 2021.

Gumbs, Alexis Pauline. *M Archive: After the End of the World*. Durham, NC: Duke University Press, 2018.

Hessell, Nikki. *Sensitive Negotiations: Indigenous Diplomacy and British Romantic Poetry*. Albany: SUNY Press, 2021.

King, Tiffany Lethabo. *The Black Shoals: Offshore Formations of Black and Native Studies*. Durham, NC: Duke University Press, 2019.

Lowe, Lisa. *The Intimacies of Four Continents*. Durham, NC: Duke University Press, 2015.

Povinelli, Elizabeth. *Geontologies: A Requiem to Late Liberalism*. Durham, NC: Duke University Press, 2016.

Tuhiwai Smith, Linda. *Decolonizing Methodologies: Research and Indigenous Peoples*. London: Zed Books, 2012.

Whyte, Kyle. "Indigenous Climate Change Studies: Indigenizing Futures, Decolonizing the Anthropocene." *English Language Notes* 55, no. 1–2 (2017): 153–62.

Wynter, Sylvia. "Unsettling the Coloniality of Being/Power/Truth/Freedom: Towards the Human, after Man, Its Overrepresentation—An Argument." *CR: The New Centennial Review* 3, no. 3 (Fall 2003): 257–337.

Wynter, Sylvia, and Katherine McKittrick. "Unparalleled Catastrophe for Our Species? Or, to Give Humanness a Different Future: Conversations." In *Sylvia Wynter: On Being as Human Praxis*, edited by Katherine McKittrick, 9–89. Durham, NC: Duke University Press, 2015.

Yusoff, Kathryn. *A Billion Black Anthropocenes or None*. Minneapolis: University of Minnesota Press, 2018.

THE VICTORIAN CULTURAL DEPLOYMENT OF NEW ZEALAND

Belich, James. *Making Peoples: A History of the New Zealanders From Polynesian Settlement to the End of the Nineteenth Century*. Honolulu: University of Hawai'i Press, 1996.

———. *Paradise Reforged: A History of the New Zealanders from the 1880s to the Year 2000*. Honolulu: University of Hawai'i Press, 2002.

Butler, Samuel. *Erewhon; or Over the Range*. London: Trübner, 1872.

———. *A First Year in Canterbury Settlement*. London: Longman, Green, Longman, Roberts & Green, 1863.

Dench, Simon. "Representing the Waikato: Photography and Colonisation." *Journal of New Zealand Literature* 29, no. 2 (2011): 66–88.

Doré, Gustave, and Blanchard Jerrold. *London. A Pilgrimage.* 1872. New York: Benjamin Blom, 1968.

Elliott, Chris. "The Needle and the New Zealander: Cleopatra's Needle as Memento Mori for Empire." *Aegyptiaca: Journal of the History of Reception of Ancient Egypt*, no. 5 (2020): 434–45.

Fermanis, Porscha. "Brexit, *Erewhon*, and Utopia." *Historical Reflections* 47, no. 2 (Summer 2021): 91–104.

Grey, Sir George. *Polynesian Mythology, and Ancient Traditional History of the New Zealand Race, as Furnished by Their Priests and Chiefs.* London: John Murray, 1855.

Macaulay, Thomas. "Review, *The Ecclesiastical and Political History of the Popes of Rome, during the Sixteenth and Seventeenth Centuries,* by Leopold Ranke." 1840. In *Critical and Historical Essays, Contributed to The Edinburgh Review in Three Volumes*, 207–54. London: Longman, Brown, Green, and Longmans, 1848.

Ministry for Culture and Heritage. "Read the Treaty." Last modified June 20, 2020. Available at New Zealand History, http://nzhistory.govt.nz/politics/treaty/read-the-treaty /english-text.

New Zealand Settlements Act 1863.Vict. Reginæ. no. 8 (1863).

NINETEENTH-CENTURY LITERATURE, CLIMATE STUDIES, AND ECOLOGY

Anderson, Katharine. *Predicting the Weather: Victorians and the Science of Meteorology*. Chicago: University of Chicago Press, 2005.

Coughlin, Maura, and Emily Gephart, eds. *Ecocriticism and the Anthropocene in Nineteenth-Century Art and Visual Culture*. London: Routledge, 2020.

Gold, Barri J. *Energy, Ecocriticism and Nineteenth-Century Fiction: Novel Ecologies*. Cham, Switzerland: Palgrave Macmillan, 2021.

Griffiths, Devin, and Deanna K. Kreisel. "Introduction: Open Ecologies." *Victorian Literature and Culture* 48, no. 1 (2020): 1–28.

Hensley, Nathan. *Forms of Empire: The Poetics of Victorian Sovereignty*. Oxford: Oxford University Press, 2016.

Hensley, Nathan, and Philip Steer, eds. *Ecological Form: System and Aesthetics in the Age of Empire*. New York: Fordham University Press, 2019.

Marsh, George Perkins. *Man and Nature; Or, Physical Geography as Modified by Human Action*. New York: Charles Scribner, 1864.

Miller, Elizabeth Carolyn. "Climate Change and Victorian Studies: Introduction." *Victorian Studies* 60, no. 4 (2018): 537–42.

———. "Dendrography and Ecological Realism." *Victorian Studies* 58, no. 4 (2016): 696–718.

———. *Extraction Ecologies and the Literature of the Long Exhaustion*. Princeton: Princeton University Press, 2021.

Parkins, Wendy, ed. *Victorian Sustainability in Literature and Culture*. London: Routledge, 2018.

Steer, Philip. "The Climates of the Victorian Novel: Seasonality, Weather, and Regional Fiction in Britain and Australia." *PMLA* 136, no. 3 (2021): 370–85.

Taylor, Jesse Oak. *The Sky of Our Manufacture: The London Fog in British Fiction from Dickens to Woolf*. Charlottesville: University of Virginia Press, 2016.

VICTORIAN LONDON, (SUB)URBANIZATION, AND THE FOG

Barratt, Nick. *Greater London: The Story of the Suburbs*. London: Random House, 2012.

Bilston, Sarah. *The Promise of the Suburbs: A Victorian History in Literature and Culture*. New Haven: Yale University Press, 2019.

———. "'Your Vile Suburbs Can Offer Nothing But the Deadness of the Grave': The Stereotyping of Early Victorian Suburbia." *Victorian Literature and Culture* 41, no. 4 (2013): 621–42.

Brimblecombe, Peter. *The Big Smoke: A History of Air Pollution in London since Medieval Times*. London: Methuen, 1987.

Corton, Christine L. *London Fog: The Biography*. Cambridge, MA: Belknap Press of Harvard University Press, 2015.

Georgiou, Dion. "Leisure in London's Suburbs, 1880–1939." *London Journal* 39, no. 3 (2014): 175–86.

Howard, Luke. *The Climate of London, Deduced from Meteorological Observations, Made at Different Places in the Neighbourhood of the Metropolis*. Vol. 1. London: W. Phillips, 1818.

Russell, Francis Albert Rollo. *London Fogs*. London: Edward Stanford, 1880.

White, Jerry. *London: The Story of a Great City*. London: Andre Deutsch, 2010.

SELECTED LATE VICTORIAN APOCALYPTIC, DISASTER, AND SPECULATIVE FICTIONS

Armstrong, Charles Wicksteed. *The Yorl of the Northmen; or, the Fate of the English Race, Being the Romance of a Monarchical Utopia*. London: Reeves & Turner, 1892.

Benson, Robert Hugh. *Lord of the World*. London: Sir Isaac Pitman & Sons, 1907.

Fawcett, Edward Douglas. *Hartmann the Anarchist; or, The Doom of the Great City*. London: Edward Arnold, 1893.

Griffith, George. *The Angel of the Revolution: A Tale of the Coming Terror*. London: Tower, 1893.

———. *Olga Romanoff, or the Syren of the Skies: A Sequel to the Angel of the Revolution*. London: Tower, 1894.

Grove, W. *The Wreck of a World*. London: Digby and Long, 1889.

Jefferies, Richard. *After London; Or, Wild England*. London: Cassell, 1885.

Shiel, M. P. *The Purple Cloud*. London: Chatto & Windus, 1901.

———. *The Yellow Danger*. London: Grant Richards, 1898.

Watson, Henry Crocker Marriott. *The Decline and Fall of the British Empire; or, The Witch's Cavern*. London: Trischler, 1890.

Wells, H. G. *The War of the Worlds*. London: William Heinemann, 1898.

THE DOOM OF THE GREAT CITY

William Delisle Hay

THE DOOM OF
THE GREAT CITY

TAPUAEHARURU, TAUPO, N.Z.,[1]
February 2, 1942.

MY DEAR GRANDCHILDREN.

It is with feelings of no little pleasure that I take up my pen on this my eighty-fourth birthday, and sit down to write to you collectively. I am about to give effect to a narrative that has been long desired on your part, as it has been long promised on mine, for I feel that if delayed any longer, it may be that I shall pass away without having told it. But first, you will be glad to

---

1. Taupō is a town on the northeastern shore of Lake Taupō, New Zealand's largest lake, in the central part of the North Island. It is now the most significant urban area of the Taupō District. Prior to European settlement, the region was known as Tapuaeharuru, "the place of echoing footsteps." Tapuaeharuru is still associated with various geographical features, including Tapuaeharuru Bay and Tapuaeharuru Stream as well as the Tapuaeharuru marae. Hay's geographical marker likely refers to Tapuaeharuru Bay.

hear that I am still hale and hearty; and how could it be otherwise, living as I do in the most beautiful climate of the world, surrounded with every comfort, and content to bear my weight of years, living again in the joys and pleasures of the numerous family with which I have been blessed? And what a family it is, to be sure, when you come to think of it! There were no less than forty-three of them, old and young, big and little, who came to bid "Grandfather" good morning to-day, and to wish him all the customary felicitations; and then, too, what a pile of letters have I had from all of you who are at a distance in your various homes scattered over Australasia! We have had quite a fête all the morning, turning the assemblage to a profit by setting everyone to work at picking fruit in the peach-orchards and orangeries, which is just in proper condition for market; and splendid fun there was, I can assure you, and no little flirtation either among the youngsters. So you see that, at any rate here in Zealandia, we keep to our old-fashioned ways of combining business with pleasure. My *great*-granddaughter, little Laura, who, as you know, is my constant companion, acted as mistress of the ceremonies, and very well, I must say, did she perform her part. At dinner, after they had drunk my health and I had responded, it was little Laura who stood up and proposed the toast of "Our absent friends, all round Lake Taupo,"—which I need not say was drunk enthusiastically. But I will not go further into these details, for I have set myself to write about another and far different subject.[2]

2. See note 12 in the introduction for more on the ambiguity of "absent friends" in the novella.

It was after they had all gone—some to catch the last train, and others to take one or other of the lake steamers, which all depart from Tapuaeharuru before sunset—that Laura came to me and, standing demurely before me with her hands crossed behind, made this pretty little speech, in which I dare say she had been carefully coached by her elders:—

"Dear Grandpapa," she said, "your children, grand-children, and great-grandchildren, who love and revere you so much, earnestly and humbly implore you to tell them the story of the GREAT EVENT of your life."

And then the dear little puss kissed me and ran away.

Well, of course I was a little shocked, for you know what my feelings have always been upon this subject; but I cannot say I was wholly unprepared for such a request. Hints have often reached me from many of you to the same effect, and particularly of late have I been admonished to break the silence I have so long imposed upon myself. I am one of the very few survivors now living, of the greatest calamity that perhaps this earth has ever witnessed, and there are doubtless many besides yourselves who would be glad to hear all I have to say about it. Sixty years ago to-day it is since the event happened, and for nearly the same number of years I have forborne to speak or write anything referring to it, in the endeavour to cloud my memory, if I might, by so doing. It was from the same reason that I came here so many years ago—came to what was then almost a solitude, almost a virgin wilderness, though now one of our most populous rural districts. But the fateful remembrance of that long-ago catastrophe is still as fresh in my mind as it was fifty-nine years back, and even now, as I recall the scenes I witnessed, and marshall my recollections for you, nature recoils in horror, and I shudder at the task before me.

I shall confine myself simply to narrating so much as fell directly within my own observation—which is what you desire, I think—for the full accounts are matters of common information; while your histories will tell you, better than I could, of preceding events, and more particularly of those great changes which followed and partly resulted from the stupendous accident.

To-day, besides being my birthday, is a sad and solemn anniversary, commemorative to the whole world of an awful fatality, and carrying me, who was myself a partaker in it, back to the dread event now buried under sixty years of time. It has always been my practice to spend the night of the 2nd of February in prayer, in meditation, and in communion with Nature in her calmest and most peaceful aspects; to-night I shall spend it in transcribing my terrible reminiscences for you, my grandchildren. Coming from me, your progenitor, and from an actual eyewitness, this relation will bear to you a more vivid reality, though it is probable I can tell you nothing that you have not already learnt through other sources. I am sitting in my comfortable little study, or "libery," as Laura calls it, surrounded by my books, my collections of objects of art and science and natural history, and the numberless little things that by reason of their various associations become priceless relics to an old man. Everything speaks to me of love, of affectionate regard, and of the dear home ties that through all these years have grown up around me here. The French windows are open, and through them comes just a breath of sweet-scented air, just a soft whiff of summer wind, that faintly stirs the honeysuckle and clematis and creepers that twine along the verandah trellis. I look out through the dusky branches of beautiful trees across the fields below, and catch a glimpse of our famous lake sleeping in the moonlight, and the dim outlines of the distant hills beyond. All this tells of peace, of calm rest, and well-earned happiness. And yet as I sit and muse, things present grow obscure; I am again a young man just entering upon the battle-field of life, striving with poverty, struggling with a crowd of others. I am transported back to the land of my birth across the intervening ocean; a land of chill and sour skies, where the sun has forgotten how to shine; a land of frost and rain, of mist and snow. I am young, but I am scarcely hopeful, for I am oppressed with many cares; I live amid noise and bustle, amid a throng of idlers and workers, good men and bad, rich and poor; I work hard at employment that demands my best energies and absorbs my young strength, and that yields me but scant repayment; I dwell shut in by bricks and mortar, and crushed by stony hearts; I am one among many, a single toiler among the millions of London!!

At the commencement of the fateful year 1882, my widowed mother, my sister, and I, dwelt together in London. I was a merchant's clerk, and had been so for several years, ever since my father's death, by depriving us of the means of existence, had altered my prospects from university life and a learned profession *in posse* to business and a high stool *in esse.*[3] My mother, and my sister, who was some years younger than I, had accompanied me to London, when it was settled that I should go into the counting-house of a merchant to whom I had been introduced by a mutual friend. There was a little money in hand, but very little, and we were glad to accept an offer that was made us. This was that we should inhabit the basement floor of a large building in the very heart of the City, receiving our accommodation free of rent and taxes, in consideration of taking care of the rest of the house, which was divided into offices and board-rooms. Here we had lived for some half-dozen years, up to the time I am writing of. My income had been fifty pounds a year at first, and was now augmented to eighty: to this was added forty pounds a year, being a sum allowed to my mother by some of her relations. Latterly my sister had begun to add a few shillings every week to the general stock by fine needlework, so that we were more comfortable than we were at first. But this united income, that was now something short of £150 per annum, was little more than sufficient to provide us with the bare necessities of existence, while every day things seemed to be growing dearer. To us, who had been accustomed all our lives before to all the comforts and little luxuries of modest competence, our straitened means were a sore trial, while a residence in the murky atmosphere, the dingy gloom, and the incessant roar of the City, was a piteous exchange from the sweet

3. *in posse*: in possibility; *in esse:* in actuality

pastoral quiet of my father's pleasant rural vicarage. I think our great and absorbing affection for one another supported my mother under all our difficulties, and enabled my sister and me to become pretty well reconciled to the dismal change. We had but few friends in London, for neither our means nor our mode of life were compatible with visiting or receiving visitors. Still we were tolerably happy in each other's society, occasionally recreating ourselves with a trip to the suburbs, or a visit to a theatre. Of the three, I was the only one who showed discontent. I was restless in spirit, and chafed under the irksome restraints of my position. I was passionately fond of the country and country pursuits, and wearied unutterably of the monotonous drudgery of my City life, which I likened to the "hard labour" of a prison; moreover, I endured constant torture of mind at the sight of my dear ones undergoing hardship, which, despite my most ardent efforts I was powerless to relieve, for, in the words of the Scottish poet, Burns:—

> "In many a way, and vain essay, I courted fortune's favour, O,
> Some cause unseen still stept between, to frustrate each
>   endeavour, O;
> Sometimes by foes I was o'erpowered, sometimes by friends
>   forsaken, O,
> And when my hope was at the top, I still was worst mistaken, O."[4]

4. Robert Burns, "My Father Was a Farmer" (1784).

And there were other causes around us, that, to my then high spirit and carefully nurtured mind, increased the loathing I felt at our whole situation in life. Such was the position of your grandfather at the eventful epoch of 1882.

I do not think you will find it easy to realize the monstrous proportions of the "Great City." For miles and miles around us on every side were streets and squares and endless ranks of houses, ever extending outwards, and absorbing suburb after suburb beneath stone and brick. The population—some four millions in number—was a nation in itself, and, like nations, the population of London had its individual characteristics. The tendency of modern times has been to curtail the inordinate increase of large cities, and you can best picture London to your minds by supposing an aggregation of our towns and cities, seaports and villages, massed together in one vast conglomeration along the banks of the ancient Thames. Various parts of London had their own distinctive peculiarities, differences in both body and spirit, so to speak. There was a wide contrast in the city of splendid mansions at the West End, for instance, and the factories and artisans' dwellings at the East; while the tone and sentiment in politics, religion, or taste, was strongly adverse in such opposite quarters as Chelsea and Whitechapel; just as the manners and customs of Mayfair differed from those of Walworth.[5] The quarter where we lived, "The City," was a large

5. Chelsea is an affluent southwestern area of London; Whitechapel is a district of East London known in the Victorian period for its poverty and overcrowding. At least some of the eleven Whitechapel murders (1888–91)

central area, being the portion of London devoted exclusively to business of every kind; it was the great emporium of the vast commerce of the country, the universal mart or exchange of Britain.[6] By night the "City" was but sparsely populated, while in the day-time the press and throng in every corner of it was something prodigious. But descriptions of London are plentiful, and every school-boy is familiar with them, while much also has been written about its inhabitants at that period; yet I would fain add something to what has been said. It was the opinion I formed at the time, and the opinion I still continue to hold, that London was foul and rotten to the very core, and steeped in sin of every imaginable variety. I was far from being a purist then, and yet I thought so; judge if I should not think so now far more strongly, when simplicity and openness of manners, truth, and honesty, are of a verity the inheritance of my children's children. Utterly unversed in open vice, from the very nature of your surroundings and bringing up, you could not contemplate the Londoners of those days without a feeling of disgust and loathing springing up within you. And yet London was esteemed as a great centre of religion; hundreds of Christian sects, enthusiastic and sincere,

---

have been attributed to the famous but unidentified killer, Jack the Ripper. Walworth is a district of south London, included within the Borough of Southwark that saw significant suburban expansion in the latter part of the nineteenth century. Mayfair is a very wealthy, expensive area of West London, near the eastern part of Hyde Park, and part of the City of Westminster.

6. "The City," often referred to as "the Square Mile" designates "the City of London," one of the boroughs (1.12 square miles) that constitute the vast metropolis of London and includes the central business district.

existed within it, and among their votaries were doubtless many who acted upon the principles they professed. They were followers of false gods, perhaps, and, indeed, so we now esteem them; but what of that? Pagan piety and Pagan virtue are piety and virtue still. I might write a long essay upon the singular anomalies of that old-world city, but such is not my present purpose; yet something I will add of what I saw around me to incline me to the belief in the black enormity of London sin.

I was in business, and business I found was an elaborate system of fraud, chicanery, and deceit. He was esteemed an upright man who never broke the *letter* of the law, no matter how he might tamper with its *spirit*, while morality and honest principle in commerce were abstractions of which the law took little notice, and business men less. He was called "smart," and "a sharp, sound, practical man," who knew how to take advantage of others, and who could enrich himself by impoverishing his fellows in "fair business." In the learned professions—so called— things were much the same. The laws were good, though inordinately cumbrous, and lawyers administered them for their own advantage, and at the expense of their unhappy clients. The law was a terrible engine of justice, but its intricate machinery was clogged with rusty "precedents," and could not be got to move without a liberal oiling in the shape of fees. Hence arose the saying, that the law had one interpretation for the rich, and another altogether for the poor. The medical profession was conducted upon similar principles; the doctor—if he knew how—would keep his patient ill in order to increase his fees, and making suffering and death his daily sport, traded upon them for his own profit. Clergymen and ministers of religion, whether belonging to the State Church or to independent bodies, made "the cure of souls" a means of livelihood; they quoted the maxim, "the labourer is worthy of his hire," applying its point to themselves; they kept alive "religious feeling" among the masses by incessant and endless quarrels among themselves on points of dogma and doctrine, extorting money in the cause of "truth" from the public, and either keeping it themselves or squandering it in various foolish and useless ways. And they made one religion for the rich and another for the poor, as anyone might learn by comparing a sermon preached before a fashionable congregation with one delivered to paupers. The merest infraction of moral integrity in one of the humbler classes was visited as intolerable; among the rich and high-born sin flourished under the hallowing sanction of religion, and vice luxuriated in the shadow of the Church. Purity of life was a simple impossibility, and chastity of soul would have been sought for in vain amongst Londoners. Theatres, music-halls, and similar institutions, appealed to the most depraved appetites; people flocked to gaze admiringly at a fashionable courtesan and her attendant harlots, or thronged to listen to obscene and filthy songs, or to witness indecent exhibitions, especially if these involved the risk of life or limb to the performers. Money flowed into the treasuries when such were the inducements, and eager rivalry in their production was the inevitable consequence. Clergymen, aristocrats, and art professors joined in extolling the stage as "the educator of public taste," while young girls crowded to enter the ballet as the proper road to a life of delightful immorality. The press groaned daily under the weight passing through it of novels which tinctured absolute crimes with poetry and romance, which clothed the worst sensuality in the white robes of innocence, and which taught and argued in favour of every vice. Serial journals adapted to every class, rested their claims to attention on the obscenity, scurrility, or blasphemy of their pages, disguised under a film of moral platitude. Such were some of the causes at work, here were some of their immediate results. Among the higher ranks of society immorality was so common as to excite but small attention; frequent divorce suits proved this; scandalous disclosures of high life were of common occurrence; they gratified the public taste while serving to show the deeper depths below.[7] Pleasure-seeking being the only employment of the wealthy and governing class, they elevated it into a "cult," and wearied with the tameness of mere harlotry, gluttony, and show, brought "art" to their aid and invented "æstheticism" as a cloak for higher flights of sin. The men of the "upper ten thousand" were trained from their cradles for a life of sensuous enjoyment. They held themselves aloof from commoner clay as from an inferior race, and they looked upon inordinate luxury as their paramount right. In their code of honour the payment of just debts had no place, unless the debt were contracted by gambling among their fellows. The "golden youth" were banded

7. The Matrimonial Causes Act of 1857 shifted marriage litigation from the jurisdiction of the ecclesiastical courts to the civil courts, in effect basing marriage on a contract instead of a sacrament and increasing access to divorce.

together into social guilds, bearing imbecile insignia, and using mysterious passwords, whose vicious meaning only the initiate might know. They had peopled a whole suburb with the villas of their concubines, whom the stage and the streets had furnished, while their elders sought amusement from almost infantile charms. Strange and unnatural were the crazes and fashions that pervaded this society: wearied with dissipation carried to excess, they were ever seeking new varieties, new emotions, new vices; they worshipped beauty, but it was not the beauty of created Nature, but that of art—and such art!—that most enchanted them. Ladies were divided into two "mondes," the proper and the improper, but it was by no means easy to define the exact limits of either grade. The Phrynes of the period held their court and received adoration from the men,[8] though not recognised by their high-born sisters; yet these were eager to copy the manners, dress, and accomplishments of the courtesan, styling themselves "professional beauties," or veiling their hyper-passionate sensibilities under the pseudonym of "intensity;" while matrimony, even among the most externally decorous, was as much a matter of business as downright mercenary prostitution. The members of this highest rank lived in the very perfection of luxuriousness; their mansions, equipages, and servants, all were on a scale of magnificence as great as could be compassed. Dresses and furniture were splendid and costly. They fared sumptuously

8. Phryne was an ancient Greek hetaira, or courtesan, who became extremely wealthy and was put on trial for impiety, at which she was acquitted after allegedly baring her breasts for the jury.

every day. Poverty was carefully excluded from their view, and came not within their cognisance, and ultra-extravagance was commended from the pulpit as a means of wisely diffusing wealth, and as an "encouragement to trade." It was said that the spendthrift vanities and caprices of the wealthy were a source of good, promoting industry, and developing arts and sciences among the workers; "wherefore," said these reasoners, "lavish and profuse prodigality is the commendable duty of the rich, as thereby they foster trade and benefit those who minister to their enjoyment." When such theories were generally received, it is needless to say that politicians were blind to comparisons drawn from the history of the latter days of Rome, of Venice, or of Bourbon France. And this state of things had, of course, its dire and disastrous effects upon all grades of society below. People of the next rank, whose wealth had been gained from other sources than that of passive hereditary accumulation, busied themselves in the endeavour to gain admission within the pale of "polite society;" they sought to imitate with exactness every eccentricity of the nobles, and courted ruin to effect their purpose. A step lower, and the same procedure was invested with the grotesque addition of "vulgarity." This abstraction consisted mainly, as I conceived, in a lack of "refinement:" it meant a want of ease and inherent use in forms of speech, manners, and usages; it con-veyed the idea of eagerness where cold indifference should have been felt; or it displayed a sense of actual pleasure, where *blasé* and captious disdain ought only to have been manifested. Throughout the great masses of the middle class, so styled, there beat the mighty pulse of London life. In this section was contained business and professional men of every degree and kind, from the wealthy banker, the opulent trader or manufacturer, and the sordid promoter of bubble companies, down to the struggling professional man, the actor, and the ignoble clerk. It was divided into a multiplicity of grades or strata, the lowest mingling with the vast democracy of labour below, the highest, by dint of golden passports, passing current among the aristocracy. It was in this division of the social system that the real life of the great city was mainly manifest; here were to be found the chief law-makers and the chief law-breakers; here was every vice most obnoxious to the senses; here, too, was to be found what was left of virtue and goodness. Down through the middle class filtered every evil of aristocratic birth, losing nothing in the process, we may be sure, save the semblance of polish and the grace of courtly elegance; while up from the lowest depths there constantly arose a stream of grosser, fouler moral putrescence, which it would be a libel on the brutes to term merely bestiality. Do not think there was *no* good in London; there was, much; but it was so encompassed and mixed with evil as to be barely recognisable; while the influences of exuberant vice were such as to warp the integrity of men's ideas of what was right, to benumb their perceptions of moral turpitude, and to lower the standard of excellence to the very mud. Besides, I only set out to tell you something of the wickedness I saw and knew and felt in London; merely a brief epitome, such as might serve to sustain the view I propounded of the guilt of that city. Have I said enough, my grandchildren? But a few words more, and I pass to the dread narrative itself.

There are some of our modern essayists who argue that "London was not such a bad place after all!" There are others, more profound, who yet are blinded by their pity for the sufferers in the fearful tragedy, to such a degree that they fail to see the odious colours of the evil that lies hidden behind the awful pall. Sadly, solemnly, grievingly, I must repeat—the old metropolis of England harboured Vice and Sin as its dearest, most cherished inhabitants. Evil! It was surely seen in the crowded police-courts; it was surely seen in the public-houses that stood thick on every street, in the infuriate or imbecile wretches who thronged their bars, in the thousand victim-votaries of Bacchus who reeled daily and nightly to and fro among them,[9] in the huge extent of the traffic in strong drink, in the potency of "the trade" as a political engine, and in the intemperate and misdirected zeal of "temperance" advocates; it was seen most flagrantly on the "day of rest"—a day of horrors to sober citizens—when crowds of the democracy pervaded suburbs, parks, and streets, flooding them with a riotous mob, making day and night hideous with the roaring of licentious songs, swearing and obscenity, turning for inspiration to the public-house—their only refuge—and not to the church, and holding nothing and nobody sacred from their ruffianly horse-play and outrageous mischief; why, certain great thoroughfares—notably on the Surrey side—were perilous for decent pedestrians after dark on any night, but especially on Sundays, and the lady had need of stout protectors

9. Bacchus: Roman god of wine, vegetation, fertility, agriculture, and revelry, also known by the Greek name Dionysus.

who ventured to encounter the gangs of blatant ruffians that asserted supremacy within them. Prostitution—I do not like to enlarge upon such a topic, but I must if I am to paint the picture faithfully—prostitution flourished so abundantly in London as scarcely to be looked upon as a vice at all, except by the most rigorous.[10] Women of this class haunted the busier streets at all hours of the day, while evening drew them forth in legions, into all parts where pleasure-seekers congregated. Nor were they confined to the streets: they thronged into every place of entertainment, music halls were specially devoted to their interests, at casinos and dancing rooms they were constant attendants; certain theatres—by no means inferior ones—were little better than brothels behind the scenes, while even churches were invaded by these daughters of the horseleech. They, too, had their social organisations, their infinite variety of cliques, their nice dividing-lines, their numerous distinctions; there was a wide gulf between the concubine of a wealthy patrician—herself, perhaps, the nominal lessee, manageress, and leading actress of a popular theatre—and the coarse creature who haunted the purlieus of Ratcliffe Highway;[11] while the

10. The first of the Contagious Diseases Acts was originally passed in 1864, authorizing police officers to arrest women suspected of engaging in prostitution. Suspected women were subjected to compulsory examinations for venereal diseases and could be confined to a lock hospital for the duration of their recovery or sentence.
11. The Ratcliffe Highway is a prominent road in the East End of London. In the nineteenth century, it was known for violence and crime, including the infamous Ratcliffe Highway murders in December 1811.

strata between these two extremes were of endless diversity. Several reasons there were for the growth of this shocking sin in London; a necessary evil in great towns, it had here reached extraordinary limits as an outcome of a false social system, as a result of unwise Governmental regulations, partly owing to the uncurbed licentiousness of the men, and perhaps due most particularly to the inordinate passion for dress that had eaten up the whole minds of the women of that age. Was this no evil? Feminine indulgence in extravagance of attire was the bane of London at that era. Ladies of the wealthy classes placed no bounds upon their love of dress, and women of every rank imitated those above them. London women, young and old, rich and poor, comely and ugly, were prepared to sacrifice fathers, brothers, husbands, relatives and friends, their homes, religion, consciences, virtue and honour—everything, in short—so long as they could flaunt in gorgeous costumes. And men were human then as now, and not too scrupulous in London, as I have said; so what wonder if prostitution flourished rampantly, while Chastity laid down her head and died! Evil!— one seemed to see it everywhere! In those latter days there had been past years of terribly bad weather, destroying harvests, and adding to the iniquity of the land-system of the country a very close cause of distress for all agriculturists; there had been long and severe depression in trade, augmented by the fact that the manufacturing industry of the country was fast going from her, owing to the want of public spirit and the avaricious selfishness that had supplanted the old British feeling, owing also to contin- ual strife between capital and labour. Such distress as was then felt throughout the rural districts of the United Kingdom had seldom before been equalled; it reacted upon the urban populations, and peculiarly on that of London; every profession, trade, or mode of earning money was over-crowded in its ranks and was curtailed in its action; while, if positive destitution overtook the already existing poor, it also touched ranks that had been heretofore far removed from its approach; extensive emigration palliated but could not cure the disease; and the piteous efforts of the thousands who were struggling with adversity in manifold paths of life were something sad to see, sad to remember. Two trades alone seemed to gain where others lost. The sale and consumption of intoxicating drink attained frightful proportions; the traffic that women offered in themselves appeared daily on the increase; both the publican and the prostitute flourished and grew fat. Was not this an appalling spectacle? Yet there was money in London; for the swollen city was at once the richest and the poorest in the world: side by side with the direst degradation of poverty there existed the superbest opulence. And, you will ask, was there then no charity?—had religion no practical work to do? As it seemed to me, looking on the surface and at what was public, religion was occupied with priestly dreams of heaven and of hell, with the building of churches and the multiplication of chapels, with sectarian strife and conflicting dogmas, with cumbrous "proofs" of itself, and with proselytising in distant lands. The poor asked for dinners, and religion handed them divinity; the rich sought pleasure, and were offered purgatory. Occasionally, some hysterical "revival" gave a brief frenzied interest to a particular creed, and left only well-filled asylums as a memento on its subsidence. This was not the religion that London wanted in those days. And charity—it was curiously understood and diabolically practised in its public aspects. Mendicancy was a misdemeanour by law, and paupers were treated worse than felons. The rich man grudgingly doled a meagre crumb from his abundance, denying himself no jot or tittle of his accustomed enjoyment, whatever the misery that cried to him for aid; the wealthy trader placed his name high upon subscription lists, and booked the sum he gave among his outlay for advertisements. Societies were formed, cursed with legal strength and status, to "organise" public benefactions, to divert private benevolence into their own channels, to steal ninepence from every shilling that was given for the poor, to stamp out poverty by oppressive measures, and to drive and grind the poor man down into a moral—hell! Such were the public charities of London; yet there were deeds of love and kindness done in the obscurity of that city, that breathed the true spirit of the religion erst preached on the shores of Galilee;[12] and it was often the poor man who was his fellow's best and only benefactor. God knows what it all might have come to under a different train of circumstances; even the lamb-like reverence for his "superiors" of the Briton might have been worn out at last. Already Republicanism was whispered in the public-houses, and Socialism was not unknown in London, though these were chiefly of exotic growth;

12. See Jesus's sermons on the shore of Galilee in the opening of the fifth chapter of *The Gospel According to St. Luke.*

while there were men of a different type—men who dared to think for themselves, who looked for the coming of some social cataclysm, and who were heard to compare the "Great City" to those Cities of the Plain that the old Biblical legend tells of as being destroyed by fire from heaven.[13]

Enough! Even a great-grandfather's garrulity must be checked in its reminiscent flow.

On the lst of February, 1882, I left business early, about half-past three in the afternoon, if I remember aright, and went home. The next day being my birthday, I had resolved, with my employer's permission, to make it a holiday; and in order that we might all enjoy it to the best advantage, a little excursion had been planned among us. My mother, my sister, and I, had agreed to accept the invitation of some of our few friends, and to go out to their house on the evening of the 1st, remaining with them until late on the following day. As our friends resided in a locality called Lordship Lane, not far from the suburb of Dulwich, we anticipated no little pleasure from the excursion, and it was consequently with feelings of delighted expectation that I hurried home from business that afternoon, to carry off my two dear ones with me on our projected visit.[14] But our plans were

13. Hay alludes to the cities of Sodom and Gomorrah. See specifically *Genesis* 18:20-19-29. Sodom and Gomorrah, as well as Admah, Zeboiim, and Zoar, make up the five "cities of the plain" referenced in Hebrew and Christian scriptures and the Qur'ān.

14. Lordship Lane is an ancient thoroughfare and main road in East Dulwich, a suburb in Southeast London, part of the Borough of Southwark. Please consult the selection from *Bacon's Library Map of London and*

overthrown by the horrible state of the weather. For weeks before, London had been stifled in a fog of varying density, but that afternoon it had grown so dense that my mother did not like to venture through it, especially since of late there had been tales about of accidents occurring from this cause, and my sister of course could not leave our mother. However, the two dear creatures had prepared everything for my departure, and were determined that I should go off alone; they were also extremely anxious that I should, if invited to do so, remain the second night at the Forresters', as my intimacy with young Wilton Forrester was likely to be of great service to me, and my good mother was anxious for me to "cultivate the friendship," as she said. I was much disappointed at their determination not to go, and would fain have stopped myself, but maternal counsels prevailed, and I set off. I found my way, not without considerable difficulty, to the railway station at Ludgate Hill. Everything was wrapped in murky gloom, though it wanted quite an hour of sunset, and the gas-lamps that were alight all day were wholly insufficient to penetrate the cloudy atmosphere with their sickly lights. I got into a train that went in my direction, and congratulated myself with the thought that I should soon be out of the worst of the fog, at any rate. I do not remember whether anyone ever attempted to write a history of London fogs, their gradual rise and progress, or gradual increase in duration and density, up to their terrific culmination; but such an

---

Suburbs (1877) in appendix E for relative locations of Lordship Lane, Dulwich, and other areas of geographic interest in the novella.

essay would form a deeply interesting one.[15] A London fog was no mere mist: it was the heavy mist, in the first place, that we are accustomed to in most latitudes, but it was that mist super-charged with coal smoke, with minute carbonaceous particles, "grits" and "smuts," with certain heavy gases, and with a vast number of other impurities. It was chiefly the result of the huge and reckless consumption of coal carried on over the wide-extending city, the smoke from which, not being re-consumed or filtered off in any way, was caught up and retained by the vapour-laden air. The fog was the most disagreeable and dan-gerous of all the climatic sufferings that Londoners had to bear. It filled the nostrils and air-passages of those who breathed it with soot, and choked their throats and lungs with black, gritty particles, causing illness and often death to the aged, weakly, and ailing; it also caused headaches, and oppression, and all the symptoms that tell of the respiration of vitiated air. Lon-doners were well accustomed to the inconvenience of these fogs, and looked upon them in the light of a regular institution, not caring to investigate their cause with a view to some means of mitigating them. The fog in the city had been known from time immemorial, especially in those districts lying near to the river, or to localities that had originally been marshes; but it was only of late years that the recurrence of fogs during autumn, winter, and spring, had assumed such alarming proportions. Even twenty

15. Hay may reference Francis Albert Rollo Russell's popular pamphlet, *London Fogs* (London: Edward Stanford, 1880). See also Luke Howard's *The Climate of London* (London: W. Philips, 1818, 1820).

years before the period I am writing of, the fog was seldom so thick and foul in character, or it was so only over very limited areas; while if it continued for more than a few hours at a time, that was considered a fact to be severely commented upon. But the plague had increased in severity of late—so much so, that its density turned day into night, and clothed night in impenetrable obscurity; its extent was greater, involving all the districts between Hampstead and the Surrey hills, and stretching from Woolwich to Bayswater;[16] its continuance was such that weeks at a time often passed over while the detestable mantle still hung above the streets. The late years of incessant rain and cold had proved conducive to the prevalence of fogs, which now appeared in unwonted seasons with all their worst features. Besides the constant annoyance from impeded traffic, from the want of light, and from the injury to health, there were other reasons for dismay; accidents by river, rail, and road were frequent and disastrous; vessels collided upon the Thames, trains ran off the lines, and their passengers were maimed or killed; while garotters, burglars, and all the guilds of open crime, revelled in contented impunity. Yet still, no one seemed to think the "institution" other than a huge joke, and not a serious evil to be earnestly combated by science, with energy and municipal wealth for helpers.

16. Hampstead is a northwest part of the London Borough of Camden traditionally associated with intellectual and artistic activity. The Surrey hills stretch over four hundred kilometers south of London. Woolwich is a southeastern London district, part of the Borough of Greenwich. Bayswater is an area within the City of Westminster, between Kensington Gardens, Paddington, and Notting Hill.

In the train, as I was journeying through the fog, I was introduced to a new feature of the prevalent affliction—a forerunner of what was so soon to follow. Although it was too murky within the carriage, in spite of the feeble glimmer of an oil-lamp overhead, for the passengers to distinguish one another very clearly, yet conversation was carried on, perhaps all the more volubly on that account. One subject engrossed attention, and from the frequent ejaculations of dismay and manifest terror that it excited, I bent forward to listen to what was said. The principal speaker was sitting at some distance from me, but his voice rose dominant above the rest, and this is the substance of what I heard:—

"Yes, gentlemen,"—he was saying,—"the report's true enough, God help us! In fact, there's no doubt about it at all. I was down Thames Street myself today, and actually saw some of the bodies being carried along. Down Bermondsey way, in some of those crowded little streets and courts, was where it happened.[17] They say the fog got suddenly so awfully thick that you couldn't see your hand before your face. About midday I should think it was; and I can well believe it, for it was nearly as bad when I was down there, a couple of hours later. Well, they told me that in some of those streets the people were choked with the fog; regularly strangled and killed outright; men, women, and children. Some were in their shops and houses, and some were in the street, but they just dropped where they stood. I was

17. Bermondsey is a southeastern London district, part of the Borough of Southwark. During the Victorian period slums developed in Bermondsey and were often blamed on new industries, shipping, and immigration.

that scared, that when I saw them carrying a couple of bodies into a public-house, I just turned and came away as fast as I could. Some said there was hundreds dead, and others said it was not above a dozen altogether. I don't know, nobody seemed to know, the rights of it; they couldn't, you see, the fog was still so dense. But, good God! gentlemen, just fancy what it would be if the like was to happen in the City. Some were talking about gas from the sewers; I don't know anything about that, but I know it's made me so nervous that, business or no business, I go out of town to-night, and stop out till the fog clears off."

A moment later we came to a station, and the speaker got out. I set down what he had said as a gross exaggeration, as did most of my fellow travellers; still I could not help a horrid feeling of dread and foreboding coming over me. I suppose there was a good deal more conversation in the carriage, but I remember nothing of it. By-and-by we came to my station, and I left the train. Here the fog was nothing more than a light white mist; indeed, the real London fog never crossed the Surrey hills. I took my way up Lordship Lane, breathing more freely, and seeming to get inspirited at every step, so marked was the change from the heavy atmosphere I had come out of. I need not tell you of the cordial and kindly reception that I found awaiting me. The Forresters were a genial, old-fashioned family, inhabiting a comfortable, old-fashioned house standing in its own walled garden, and looking down upon the trim plastered villas that were springing up all around it. The family consisted of Mr. and Mrs. Forrester, three daughters, and the son, Wilton, who was my senior by a few years, and who was a physician, though not in practice. They were in good circumstances, but not what the world then considered rich. I had made Dr. Wilton Forrester's acquaintance some two years before under somewhat singular circumstances, which had led to my introduction to his family, and by degrees to our present intimacy. The family were very hospitable, and subsequent events, of which you are aware, showed them to be kind and warm-hearted in no common degree. On that memorable evening they gave me a most kind welcome, expressing ready disappointment at not seeing my mother and sister with me. It was agreed that in the morning Wilton and I should go into town and fetch them out; nothing short of my promise to that effect would pacify the good people. I will pass over the details of the pleasant evening that followed dinner; it was like all such evenings among an agreeable family circle. I soon saw that no tidings had reached these amiable folk relative to the rumour I had heard in the train, and I forbore to speak on the subject, as the girls were full of jokes about the fog, and well primed with a hundred amusing anecdotes of the strange predicaments that were constantly befalling people in the clouded streets. They might well laugh who were removed beyond the influence of the fog, but such was the fashion in which everyone was accustomed to treat the subject—*until that night*.

Afterwards, when Mr. Forrester, Wilton, and I were sitting over our pipes in the smoking-room, I told them the story as I had heard it. They were infinitely shocked, as may be imagined, and slightly incredulous; the affair was so novel in character, so contrary to all previous experience, that we hesitated to accept it

for truth, rather preferring to suppose that some unforeseen accident of a less unheard-of description had been the basis from
which the rumour had sprung. Naturally, we continued to talk
of nothing else, and I remember that Wilton gave us the benefit
of his scientific acquirements in our various speculations. As our
talk bore very much upon the explanation of the subject of my
narrative, I shall endeavour to recall the substance of it for you.
It began by my observing that I could not understand how the
fog—however bad it might be—could become sufficiently thick
or poisonous as to destroy life. Moreover, we had been accustomed, more or less, to London fogs ever since London existed,
and I had never heard that people had been killed by them in that
way before; the present fog had lasted since Christmas, and was
not so thick to-day as it had been sometimes previously. My argument therefore was, that as the fogs had not before been found
directly hostile to life, it was to be presumed they were not so
now, since no distinctly new element had been imported into
them. You perceive, my children, that, young and unthinking as
I was, my spirits had risen with my surroundings, and under their
influence I was inclined to take the usual Londoner's view, and
to scoff at the idea of a time-honoured nuisance turning out an
actual danger. But both my companions were of different opinion. The elder Forrester said there was clear evidence that the fog
injured health, even to the point of proving very quickly fatal to
old people, and to those who were suffering from chest complaints or pulmonary weakness of any kind. There was clear evidence that it already did do so. The statistics of the death-rate
showed this to be so beyond dispute. It was also evident to old

inhabitants of London that the fogs were becoming aggravated every year, and the injury they did was increasing in due proportion. He did not see that we were justified in supposing the fogs to have attained the worst extent of virulence, although he sincerely trusted they had; and if it was shown that they were at present directly injurious to health, and an immediate cause of death to certain invalids, it could be easily understood how the intensification of the fog would tend to the detriment of human life. Yet he was not prepared to credit the report I had heard, because it really seemed too much in the nature of a fable, and he thought such an event could scarcely happen under present existing circumstances. Although he saw the possibility of such accidents in some distant period of the future, yet he could not realise to his mind their actual occurrence now. Such was the old gentleman's opinion; meanwhile Wilton had been fidgeting in his seat, occasionally shaking his head, and giving vent to smothered ejaculations. When his father finished speaking, he said somewhat as follows :—

"The more I come to think of the rumour you have heard, the more I am inclined to admit the possibility of its entire truth. I recollect a case that was brought into hospital during the very severe fogs of a couple of winters ago.*[18] It was that of a cabman, who had suddenly pitched headlong off his seat, and was picked up dead. The cause of death was at first supposed to be fracture of the skull, and it was held that the fall had resulted from drunkenness. However, the post-mortem threw an entirely different

18. *1880. [Hay's note]

light upon the case. From it we had reason to conclude that the fall must have taken place after life was extinct, and there was no sign of any organic disease or chronic mischief to account for it. The cause of death was evident from the state of the lungs and air-passages, which were highly congested. The bronchi and tubes ramifying from them were clogged with black, grimy mucus, and death had evidently resulted from a sudden spasm, which would produce suffocation, as the lungs would not have the power in their clogged condition of making a sufficiently forcible expiratory effort to get rid of the accumulated filth that was the instrument of death. That was the only case of actual death from inhalation of London fog that I have seen myself, but there have been many others exactly similar reported."[19][†]

After some more cases of the same kind had been quoted, Mr. Forrester began speculating as to the way in which the fog might have acted in destroying life, in the instance of the people in Bermondsey. His theory was, that the air underwent some extraordinary chemical changes; that, loaded with carbon in a finely-divided condition, and with the various products of combustion, there might happen—possibly under an electrified condition of the atmosphere—a sudden increase of affinity, by which carbonic oxide would be formed in prodigious quantity. As this gas is fatal to life, every breathing thing within the area of its influence would die. But Wilton combated this opinion; he said:—

---

19. [†]Dr. Broadbent, one of the leading physicians of that day in London, also, I believe, had one or two such cases that came under my notice during the same fog. [Hay's note]

"If what you were supposing were to be possible, and were actually to happen, there would be a sudden alteration in the volume of the surrounding air; this would be sufficient, I think, to produce formidable air currents whose progress and agitation would be quite rapid enough to preserve such an admixture of oxygenated air as would prevent the ill effects to life that you are afraid of. No; I see only one way in which the fog is likely to act as a life-destroying agent—apart, that is, from its action in carrying poisonous germs and spreading epidemics, which illustrates its slower action—but as a rapid and immediate extinguisher of vitality the cause must be bronchial spasm. You see that each inspiration draws into the lungs a quantity of gritty particles; these necessarily inflame and lacerate the structures with which they are brought in contact, besides mechanically choking the passages; hence follows spasm of the bronchi, spasm of the glottis. Usually there exists the power to recover from this rapidly. Prolonged or energetic coughing brings up the cause of obstruction and relieves the muscular contraction, and the asthma or 'choking fit' is over. But suppose," continued Wilton, "such an aggravation of the fog, such an increase in its density, compression and carriage of mechanical impurity, as to make each one inspiration contain the same amount of irritative matter as do, say a score or so of inspirations at present. What would be the effect of that? There would not be the chance of a recovery; each gasp would only aggravate the distress, suffocation complete and sudden would be inevitable. That is the way in which the cabman's death was brought about; and that is the way, in my opinion, in which the Bermondsey affair took place.

"The more I study these things in my mind the gloomier become my forebodings. We do not know the laws which govern the fogs of London, because in some measure they are artificial, and so differ from other mists. We only know that they have tended to become 'worse,' as we express it, of late years. How are we to know that this intensifying has reached its limits? May not the loss of life be even more serious from this cause? It is a pity that Government, and private individuals too, have not been readier in striving after some means of abating what we have long known to be an intolerable nuisance, and what seems about to become a very grave evil. Scientists have indeed made suggestions, but no steps have as yet been taken to determine their practical utility. Perhaps this accident in Bermondsey may direct attention to the subject."

I can remember yet the indescribable thrill which passed through me during these conversations. How wonderful it seems to me, looking back upon these events, that the warning never came until too late to be of service, that the cause for alarm so shortly preceded the blow. About the very time that we were sitting talking, scenes were enacting not so far from us that——— but I must proceed regularly with my tale.

As you may guess, the horrible rumour which I had heard so circumstantially detailed, together with the conversation arising out of it later in the evening, went with me to my bed, and, impressed deeply on my mind, filled my sleep with all the wild phantasmagoria of frightful dreams. I rose in the morning feeling feverish and unrefreshed, and filled with a weird presentiment of evil that I was powerless to shake off. I drew up the blind, and looked out of the window. The sun was shining in a pale, sickly kind of way through the mist, which, however, seemed to be lightening a good deal. Towards the south one could see for a considerable distance, the mist being light and hazy; but in an opposite direction it deepened into a dense brown fog-bank, which lay along the line of the Surrey hills, completely shutting out all view beyond. I turned away with a shudder as my thoughts flew to my dear ones who were far in the depths of that hideous obscurity. Downstairs the family party was assembled for breakfast, the ladies light-hearted and full of raillery, the men depressed and anxious. There was a discordant tone in our voices, and an absent-mindedness in our manners which brought down on our heads many a light shaft of feminine wit; for both the Forresters, father and son, were, like me, oppressed with a troubled sense of something wrong, the result of our last night's talk. We were all most eager for the arrival of the morning papers, hoping they might relieve our fears, but neither the post nor the papers made their appearance. This was extraordinary, when ten o'clock came and still no tidings from the outer world had reached us. Our evident uneasiness had extended itself to the ladies, in spite of our efforts to seem cheerful, making dismal attempts at jocularity, saying that the postman must have lost his way in the fog, and so forth. But it was all to no use; a portentous gloom hung over us and refused to be lifted. At length we could bear it no longer, and making some excuse about going to see what had delayed the post we three men sallied out, and took our way down the hill in the direction of East Dulwich. Now up to this time I do not recollect that I had any actual sense of fear. A feeling, indefinable and objectless, of despondency and nervous shrinking I have already confessed to—just such an inexplicable sensation of presentiment, of *waiting* for some unknown, un-thought of horror that was lying ready to appear, but was at present shrouded from view, which everyone knows as an accompaniment to that class of dreams we call nightmare: yet I had in no sense realized the immediate approach of evil to myself or to those I loved. I think I have pretty accurately expressed the nature of my inward feelings up to the moment when the two Forresters and I commenced our walk. But every moment after that brought nearer and nearer to my mind the horrid reality of dread; fixed deeper inwardly a fuller horror as events became known and an agony of unutterable fear gradually filled every sense and thrilled every nerve within me. Aye, my grandchildren, little can you understand the utter intensity of that all-absorbing terror, which even now causes my very soul to quake within me as I write. This is no exaggeration; wait, and read the awful tale, if I can command myself to finish it.

As we came out into the high-road, we overtook a gentleman who was proceeding in the same direction as ourselves. He was a neighbour of the Forresters, and was known to them, so we fell into conversation. Like us, he had been much perturbed by the non-appearance of the postman, and he was now on his way to try and obtain tidings of him. From him we gained the first startling piece of intelligence. This gentleman had seen the "special edition" of an evening paper the previous night, and in it, he said, was an account of the accident in Bermondsey. The report said that over five hundred lives were certainly lost, but that, owing to the dense fog in the locality, and the difficulty of getting men to enter it, the exact total could not yet be known. It went on to add that although people in the adjacent district asserted the cause of the calamity to have been simply a sudden and overwhelming access of fog, this *could not* have been the true reason, *because it was contrary to all previous experience*; "wherefore," said this sapient journal, "we must suppose that a gush of foul sewer-gas, or some similar poisoning of the thick and heavy air, produced the fatal effect;" a piece of reasoning which almost moved Wilton to laughter. This is a fair illustration of how strangely fixed in the London mind was the notion that their fog was always to be, what it always *had been*, innocuous to the generality of people—an idea which had served to prevent any steps being taken in the direction of rendering it really so. Now, as we had seen reason to admit the possibility of the mere fog acting as a direct destroyer, we were sadly disheartened by this confirmation of the evil news. It is easy now to follow the train of conclusions which made our vague anxieties assume a more vivid shape.

Firstly, supposing it proved that the fog could kill an individual—and Wilton had proved that—what was to hinder its killing a number of individuals in a certain spot? and *that* was now proved to our minds. Again, if the fog could attain to such virulence over any special locality, there was no just reason for supposing that its area of destructive maleficence might not be enlarged to an almost indefinite extent. So thinking and talking, we passed on down the road towards East Dulwich.

As we entered that part of Lordship Lane which formed the main street of East Dulwich, and where such shops and public-houses as the suburb boasted were to be found, we became aware of a very great commotion going on. The fog was here somewhat denser than on the higher ground we had left, though it was still only a whitish mist. But the usually quiet street, so far as we could see through the mist, presented a most unaccustomed spectacle. People were rushing wildly to and fro, groups were gathered in the roadway, on the pavement, inside and outside of the public-houses and the shops; all seemed imbued with ungovernable and frantic excitement, and on every face might be traced the same expression, panic, terror, fear! What was the matter?

Hastily we mingled with the throng, anxiously we questioned first one and then another. None seemed to know exactly what had occurred; none were possessed of details, yet the very vague-ness of the thousand rumours lent potency to their fears, while all concurred in one frenzied outburst—THE FOG! Some told us that all access to town was shut off by an impenetrable wall of fog; others said that no person or vehicle of any kind had come out of town that morning. Some spoke of the entire cutting off of all communication with London as a temporary nuisance and a good joke, but their blanched faces and quivering lips too plainly showed the dread that was at work within them; while others there were who told of men that had essayed to penetrate the vaporous veil, and who had returned, scared and choking, to speak of dead men lying in the street whose bodies they had stumbled over, to tell of the suffocating intensity of the dreadful fog. So asking and so answered, we came to Champion Hill railway station, where a large but awestricken crowd was gathered.[20] Here we learnt the fullest details that were yet known. All traffic into and out of London was indeed suspended, or rather, had never commenced. No trains had come out from the London termini, no response had been received to signals or telegrams; while men who had started to walk into town had either never returned, or else had shortly retraced their footsteps, panting and half-strangled. Telegrams from other suburbs and outskirts of town brought intelligence of a precisely similar state of things existing in those localities. No one had come from London, no one had succeeded in entering it. Such public conveyances as were wont to start every morning with their freight of "City men," had made efforts to do so in vain. They had been forced to relinquish the attempt, owing not only to the black obscurity, but also to the unbreathable character that the fog seemed to have assumed. Crowds of men who lived in the suburbs and were employed in the City by day, thronged the stations, a dreadful panic having taken possession of them and altered their usual demeanour. Instead of the accustomed noise, bustle, and brisk hurry, white-faced groups consulted together in whispering tones; and many, utterly demoralized by excess of terror, had gone home to carry off their families to some place of greater safety. All round the "Great City" lay a wide belt of

20. Renamed East Dulwich railway station, Champion Hill railway station opened in 1868.

suburban districts, and these were now—so it seemed—
given up to confusion, peopled with panic, and invaded
with dismay. What were my feelings now? Judge for yourselves. Do you suppose I can tell you? A man came down the
station steps, as we terrified wretches cowered together below,
loudly exclaiming:—

"I tell you, it's damned nonsense; they CAN'T be all killed
in London!"

All killed! The words went to my heart like a knife. Can you
fancy the very extravagance of dread? It was mine then. Can
you imagine the utmost climax of terror? I knew it at that
moment. How I looked, what I said or did, what I thought
even, these things I know not. The awful pang had shot into
my heart and brain, had benumbed my inmost soul.

Fear! It was scarcely such a sense: I had no thought of personal danger, hardly a recollection even of the too possible fate
of those dear ones who were more to me than life; the agony that
held me then, that has pursued me through sixty years of time to
hold me now, was no common sense of fear. It was that overwhelming, all-mastering dread which men alone can know who
are on a sudden taught their own immeasurable littleness; who
are witnesses of some stupendous event, whose movement shows
the hand sublime of Nature, the supremacy of offended God!

Yes, you know now, though I knew not then, the full extent
of that hideous catastrophe: how, like the sudden overflow of
Vesuvius upon the towns below; like of yore the wings of the
angel of death had overshadowed the sleeping hosts of Assyria;
or like that yet older tale, a world had sunk beneath the waters,

so, in like manner, the fog had drawn over midnight London an envelope of murky death, within whose awful fold all that had life had died.[21]

Can you understand now the train of reasoning which led your grandfather to expatiate on all that was vile and wicked in the once-entitled "Modern Babylon"? Do you not see why I rather recall the evil and forget the good? Else were not my grief multiplied a thousandfold, my anguish of pity more absorbing? And thus reflecting, may I not look up to Heaven still reverencing Just God; still dwelling in earnest faith on the love and mercy of Him Who is the Father of His creatures?

Although our knowledge of what had actually taken place was as yet extremely vague and limited, still we were sensible that the "Great City" beyond us lay stupefied, paralysed, to all seeming devoid of life, and that at an hour—it was now approaching noon—when it was usually busiest. This was alone unparalleled and horrifying, and as minute chased minute by and still no news relieved prevailing fears, and still the horrid fever of suspense made things seem darker, so the first consternation spread and deepened until a vast wave of awful, unheard-of terror rushed

21. Mount Vesuvius, a volcano on the Gulf of Naples in Italy, has erupted numerous times but is best remembered for the eruption of AD 79 that destroyed Pompeii, Herculaneum, Oplontis, Stabiae, and other communities, killing in excess of one thousand people; "like of yore": See 2 Kings 18–19 and specifically 19:35. See also Isaiah 37:36–38. "or like that yet older tale": Hay is likely referencing the legend of Atlantis, whose people were punished with the sinking of their city for their greed and immorality, but there are various cultural myths of sunken cities, punished by deities.

back from the outskirts of London. By this time every vehicle that could be put in motion was loaded with goods and with women and children, while crowds of people of all stations and sexes were hurrying along the roads which led to the country. Whither, none knew or cared; their only anxiety was to get away beyond the influence of the LONDON FOG, which their magnified panic believed was steadily advancing outward from the town. I cannot think that my own faculties had remained unshaken amid the frenzy of fear that boiled up around me; yet the deep sense of awe that fell upon me seemed to banish all merely personal fears. By-and-by, soon after noon I think, I noticed a sensible alteration in the fog; it became lighter around us, while puffs of wind were now to be felt at short intervals. The line of mansions along the crest of Champion Hill, previously invisible from the lower ground where we were, now came out into view. I was pretty sure that the fog was becoming more tenuous—"lifting," in short. The recollection of my mother and sister came before my mind so strongly that I resolved instantly to make my way to them. I intimated my resolution to the Forresters, my companions. They did not attempt to dissuade me, but the old man wrung my hand and said, "Come back to us, my lad, if—" and he nodded and turned away. Then I passed on my road into London.

It was but a step away from the remaining groups of people collected about the railway station and the last houses of East Dulwich, and I was at once alone. My way at first lay up Champion Hill, along a road bordered by fields and gardens belonging to the mansions higher up. Once these were passed, rows of smaller dwellings lined the road which passed along the crest of the high ground to Denmark Hill, whence the streets were continuous and part of London.[22] As I came down the street that emerged upon Denmark Hill, I began to be dreadfully affected by the fog, that seemed to become worse at every step. It was very thick and dark upon the Camberwell side of the hill, and appeared to have a peculiar irritating pungency which made me cough incessantly, until I found that by muffling my nose and mouth in my woollen wrapper I was able to endure it better. After a while, either the density of the fog had greatly decreased or my throat became more callous to it, for I was able to breathe without any difficulty. At this time I was still oppressed by a feeling of unutterable awe, which absorbing presence seemed to leave no room for any other sentiment. Added to this there now came over me a terrible sense of loneliness, indescribably horrible indeed in such a situation. I traversed the foggy street, seeing objects but indistinctly at ten yards distance. I saw no living being, no faces at the shrouded windows, no passers by, no children playing in the gardens or the road; not even a sparrow fluttered past to convey to me the sense of companionship. And then the frightful, muffled stillness that seemed to hold me down in a nightmare trance; not a sound of traffic, no rattle of carriages and carts, no scream and rumble of trains, no clamour of children or costermongers, no distant hum of the

22. Denmark Hill is an area and road in Camberwell, part of the London Borough of Southwark.

midday city, no voice or whisper of a sound; not the rustling of a leaf, not the echo of a footfall, nothing to break the deathly stillness but the panting of my laboured chest and the beating of my trembling heart. Below the brow of Denmark Hill, in the street leading into Camberwell, I stumbled over something in the path. It was the body of a policeman lying stretched across the pavement. Horrified, I stooped beside him, striving to find a spark of life, but he was cold and dead. There he lay, as he had probably been struck down upon his beat, the face fixed and set, the skin of a mottled bluish cast, some black moisture hanging about the nose and lips and on the beard. It seemed to me the first realization of some horrible dream; I would have shouted for aid, but my voice sank back upon my lips and I dared not cry aloud. Hastily I fled on upon my way. Alas! horror lay thick before me, and thicker yet. As I came out into the open square called Camberwell Green I saw three cabs standing on the rank;[23] the horses had fallen and were lying dead between the shafts, while at a little distance an indistinct mass upon the sidewalk was probably the bodies of the drivers; I ventured not to approach them. I faced the road leading to London Bridge, meaning to take it; some huge object loomed up before me through the fog. Approaching, I found this to be an omnibus; but, O God!—did ever man before me witness such a sight? I supposed subsequently that this was some belated car from the Middlesex side of the river, that with its load of passengers had struggled bravely on through the

23. Camberwell Green is a 2.5-acre common-land park in Camberwell.

gathering gloom of the preceding night to this point, where it had been overtaken by the death-dealing acceleration of fog.[24] We know from the printed accounts that there was abundant evidence discovered to prove that the crisis occurred at different hours in several localities. This was the object that barred my road, seen indistinctly and weirdly in the misty light, as I suddenly came upon it. Drawn across the roadway, probably by the plunging of the horses in their last suffocative agony, it presented a spectacle more appallingly hideous than the most distempered imagination could easily picture to itself. Ah! I can see it yet, in all the vivid ghastliness that was burnt indelibly into my remembrance. The driver, and those who occupied the front seats, still sat, but not as they sat in life. The attitudes of the corpses showed the sudden agony and spasm of their deaths. The driver hung forward sustained by the belted apron, his clenched hands thrown out before him, and in one he still clutched a portion of his whip that he had broken possibly in the final struggle. On either side of him were other bodies showing too plainly the effects of the convulsion that had overpowered them. One sat still upright, his arms thrown back and grasping at the rail, his head, supported from behind, was erect and left the face in view. Oh, the insupportable horror of that dead man's look! The staring eyes, the gasping mouth, the livid skin, the strained and tortured whole. Below them lay the horses, dead in their harness; above and behind, the roof of the

24. Middlesex is a southeastern English county, almost all of which is within the area of Greater London.

vehicle that had been full-occupied with men, was now loaded with their bodies. One or two had dropped from the top and lay upon the ground below, while one hung head-downwards over the side. I could see the interior of the car where women had chiefly sat. Poor creatures! they had been coming home, perhaps, after their day's work or evening's pleasure, and now I saw them entwined together in a twisted, contorted heap, that made me fancy I could even behold the writhing, the piteous interlacing of hands, the convulsive catching at each other, and hear the choking shrieks and cries for succour that too surely here had made more dreadful the spasm and terror of sudden death.

Oh, pitying heaven! For sixty years I have prayed unceasingly that the hideous memories of that awful day might be blotted from my mind.

I turned in an excess of horror from that grim load of dead, and rather than pass by it I took another road. So great was the effect of these horrors upon my mind, so terrible was the emotion I experienced, that I pursued my way with difficulty. Sometimes I fell upon my face or upon my knees in a very frenzy of agitation, while my mind kept working in a voiceless prayer to the Supreme. Tottering and shaking in every limb I went on my way, swaying and staggering with the palsy and delirium of abject dread. Scarcely knowing what I did, I followed the tramway rails in the centre of the road, caring little in which direction they led me. But the fog, unmerciful before, had mercy to me then; its loathsome mantle shrouded numberless deadly horrors from my view, and veiled a veritable Valley of the Shadow of Death as

I passed through it.[25] Gradually I recovered in some degree from the first intensity of my emotions, and walked on, still trembling, but calmer. I kept my eyes bent upon the ground, and held along the tramway, not daring to look up in case my eyes might again encounter some fearful spectacle. Often I passed by dark objects of whose dismal character I was but too well convinced, though I avoided their inspection. Several times I saw the body of a man or of a woman lying close to the track. At length I came to a bridge; it was Vauxhall Bridge, and here I lingered for a while, listening to the sound of the waters beneath.[26] The plashing of the river was a friendly sound in my ears, the first sound that had broken the deep stillness of the fog-bound region since I had entered it; it cheered me up in some indescribable way. I passed across the bridge and again took my way onward through the streets of the silent city.

Not far from the bridge, upon the Middlesex side, I came upon another awful sign of the impartiality and completeness of the tremendous catastrophe. Close to the edge of the pavement there stood a carriage—one of those elegant and voluptuously-appointed vehicles which the wealthiest people were wont to use. The spot I had now reached was no great distance from the

25. Hay likely references Psalm 23, "The Lord is my shepherd," but he may also allude to Roger Fenton's April 23, 1855, Crimean War photograph, "Valley of the Shadow of Death," often considered one of the most famous early war photographs, which was exhibited in London.

26. Vauxhall Bridge is one of several central London bridges that traverses the Thames. Originally known as Regent Bridge, it was first built between 1809–16 as part of larger efforts to redevelop the south bank of the river.

fashionable quarter of London, where every night one might see numbers of such carriages conveying aristocratic parties to and from their residences. It seemed as though this equipage must have missed its way in the obscurity, and been brought to a stand, for one of the gorgeously-liveried flunkeys lay prone beside the door, while his fellow had fallen from his perch behind. The coachman, huddled up upon his seat, appeared as though watching his horses, which lay in a confused heap below him, their smooth and silken coats still handsome beneath the bravery of silver harness. I noticed a coronet upon the emblazoned panels, and as I looked through the window of this splendid carriage my eye was caught by the glitter of jewellery, the gleam of white skins, and the flash of bright colours. O sad, heartrending spectacle! An elderly lady reclined in a corner, while stretching forward, with arms encircling her as though imploring help, were two fair girls. The piteous agony and terror that distorted those once lovely faces was rendered more fearfully startling by the magnificence of their dress and adornments. Weak and unstrung in nerve as I was, my tears flowed at the sight of these patrician beauties, fresh from the tender frivolities of the Court or the ball-room, lying out here, the victims of that clammy, relentless fog. Again I turned and fled, but not for far, till once more my steps were arrested. And here was a strange and woeful antithesis to the last picture—one of those sights too common to be noticeable in living London, yet how infinitely, solemnly mournful in the city of the dead! Two miserable little bodies in the gutter, two poor little ragged urchins, barefooted, filthy, half-naked outcasts of the stony streets, their meagre limbs cuddled round each other in a last embrace, their poor pinched faces pressed together and upturned to heaven. To them, perhaps, death had been but release from life. What a contrast to the occupants of that carriage, not a stone's-throw off! One common doom, one common sepulchre of gloomy fog, there was for the richest and the poorest, the best and the worst alike.

I went hurriedly on, my faculties whirling confusedly with these accumulating shocks. I felt as though I were left alone on earth, and indeed I was the only living creature amid multitudes of dead that but a few hours ago had filled the houses and the streets around me with life. Why had I been left to live when Death had garnered such a mighty harvest? O London! surely, great and manifold as were thy wickednesses, thy crimes, thy faults, who stayed to think of these in the hour of thy awful doom, who dared at that terrible moment to say thy sentence was deserved? And I, a lingering survivor of thy slain, oh, pity that it should have been my task to tell of thy CORRUPTION, to bear witness to thy PUNISHMENT!

It was strange that all this while I had not felt any distinct apprehension for my mother and sister. I had not connected them in my mind with the idea of death. I had yearned to be with them when danger and alarm was all around. I longed intensely to see their dear faces, to hear their dear voices, and to lead them beyond the bounds of the ghastly metropolis; but I had some-how no realised sense of the approach of danger to them per-sonally. But now the first shadowy suspicion of what might be came into my mind; vague, it may be, yet sufficient to spur my footsteps more quickly onward. The thought that the all-pervading death could seize upon my treasures had not definitely come before my mind; such a fear was too monstrous, too appalling for me to entertain; for you know, my grandchildren, that those two darling women were all the ties I then had in the world; on them my whole affections were centred; they were the sum and substance of my life. Now that I had conceived the dim possibility of the approach of evil to them I was instantly overwhelmed by the desire to be with them. These thoughts were mingled with those terrifying emotions that I have told you were evoked by the scenes I was witnessing. Pressing my hands over my eyes to try and shut out the now more frequently recurring spectacles of death, I staggered forward till at length I came beneath the wall of Buckingham Palace. There was a slight stir in the air, and a perceptible lightening of the grimy vapours, as I turned into the space before the palace. I saw the outline of the trees in St. James's Park, and above the high façade of the palace I caught a glimpse of the flagstaff, with the drooping standard hanging almost motionless.[27] As I passed the gates a sudden dazzle of scarlet caused me to start; it was the sentry in his box. Standing upright as though in life, propped against the wall of the sentry-box, his rifle resting butt-end upon the ground, his hands crossed upon the barrel, the heavy bearskin on his brows adding to the look of stern, resolved despair that was expressed in his set and staring eyes. There he remained, steadfast in death—a dead

27. St. James's Park is a large park in central London in the City of Westminster bordered by Buckingham Palace to the West.

sentinel watching the dead. Not far in front of the gate lay the body of a woman—God knows who or what! She lay there upon her face with extended arms, her rich furs and silks dabbled in the mud, her delicately-gloved and jewelled hands vainly grasping at the stones, her painted cheek and yellow hair pressed into the mire of the gutter. Bethink you, was it not enough to unman me to pass through these familiar places in the hours of daylight, and to see nothing but a dreadful series of deaths spread out into a continuous panorama of horror before me? Aye! do you wonder now that sixty years have failed to efface these awful details from my mind? Imprinted, burnt upon my memory, such recollections must remain with me till I, too, am claimed by Death!

I think that at this juncture some kind of madness came over me. For some time past my brain had seemed to reel, sickened with its terrible impressions; yet still striving with outstretched hands to blind my sense of sight, unsteadily yet frantically I hurried forward. Down the Mall, behind terraces of palatial mansions, and through Trafalgar Square, I reached the Strand. Scarcely can I pourtray in words the dire and dismal scenes that met my vision here. From Charing Cross and onwards, I crept along, one solitary shuddering wretch, amid such a hecatomb of deathly woe, as may well defy the power of man to truthfully describe.[28] For here, where on the previous night had throbbed

28. The Mall is a road in the City of Westminster that travels between the western end of Buckingham Palace and Trafalgar Square. The Strand is a major thoroughfare in the City of Westminster that served as a main location for theaters and music halls during the nineteenth century. Trafalgar Square is a main public square in Westminster that was designed in the

hot and high the flood-tide of London's evening gaiety, was now presented to my poor fevered sight, the worst, most awful features of the whole terrific calamity. I had entered into the very heart and home of Horror itself.

Somewhere near the middle of the Strand, an impulse I can scarcely define drove me to seek refuge from the piled horrors of the street. Although it was so central a thoroughfare as to have gained for itself the cant name of "High Street, London," yet I had but little personal acquaintance with it. One place I knew slightly, a tavern-restaurant, where I had occasionally dined or supped with acquaintances. Thither I bent my steps, picking my way in shivering dread among the corpses that strewed the way— aye! strewed the pavement and the roadway so thickly, O God! so thickly! Somehow I think I must have hoped to find there friendly, sympathizing, *living* faces; I know not else why I, a lonely wanderer among those thousand mute, stricken victims, should have been seized with another soul-shaking shock, another paroxysm of maddening fear. I had entered the half-open doors of the restaurant, and passed within the bar, where still many of the gas-lamps burnt brightly, mixing with the murky daylight and adding a baleful ghastliness to the scene. No voice, no sound were there to welcome or to check me. I stood unheeded in a house of the dead. Behind the bar a heap of women's clothes huddled in a corner caught my eye: I needed not

nineteenth century with a central, commemorative statue of Admiral Nelson (Nelson's Column). Charing Cross is a junction in Westminster at which six different routes intersect.

to look more closely to see that it was a barmaid, for nearer to me was another, drawn down as though by some unseen force from behind, her hands still grasping the handles of the beer-engine, her head fallen back upon her shoulders, her body half-hanging, half-crouched upon the floor. Poor girls! The last time I had seen them—only a few days before—they had stood there in all the vanity of youth and beauty, decked with flowers, cheap jewellery, and flashy clothes, smiling on the customers they supplied, bandying "chaff" with their admirers, and listening greedily to the vapid compliments of the boozy dandies, some of whose bodies now lay prostrate at my feet. So had they been occupied up to the sudden awful moment when the FOG-KING had closed down upon his prey.[29] I dared not pass beyond the threshold of the house, yet the one rapid glance that my eye took of the scene within sufficiently impressed its details on my memory. There were the half-empty glasses upon the counter, those who had been drinking from them lying stark upon the floor; men in all the frippery of evening dress, the cigar or cigarette just fallen from their twisted lips; men in less conspicuous attire; here and there a woman or two; most of them, alas! showing too plainly by the garish ostentation of their garments the class to which they belonged; further on, in the supper-room behind, I could see the dishes and supper equipage upon the tables, while, in the chairs around them, on the floor below, and leaning across the

29. Hay's use of "the FOG-KING" may be a strange permutation of the *Punch* cartoons, including "Old King Coal and the Fog Demon," published on November 13, 1880.

tables themselves, in all the dreadful confusion of sudden death, in all the hideous contortion of paralyzed panic, were the mortal remains of those who had been sitting there joyously supping, when the hour of doom had struck. Ah! and there was one sad group that struck me more than all the rest, from which, too, they seemed to differ strangely; it was a man and a woman—boy and girl, perhaps I should rather say—who occupied the corner of a couch close to the door. Her arms were thrown around his neck, her face was pressed down into his bosom, and he, holding her to him with convulsive embrace, lay back in his seat, his strangled face upturned with such a yearning agony of entreaty for aid where aid there was none, with such expression in the glassy eye, in the parted lips, from which I fancied I could still hear issue the hoarse accents of despairing prayer and frenzied supplication, that the sight seemed to congeal the remaining life-current within me. Dizzy with affright, my whirling brain drew some strange analogy between that young man and myself, between the dead girl he clasped in his dead arms and my sister.

Again I was in the Strand, striving to pass a hideous barrier of carriages and cabs, interlocked, overturned and confounded in one still medley of death; the bodies of horses, of men, and of women intermixed in the horrible confusion. I crossed the street the better to avoid it, and came under the portals of one of the principal theatres. The doors stood open and the gaslights were flaming within; but few bodies lay about the entrance as I stepped inside, impelled by a swift fascination I was powerless to resist. I passed down the gay and glittering corridor that led into this temple of pleasure; becoming in some degree accustomed

to the sight of death, I walked unheeding past the silent, crouch-
ing forms of those who had been the guardians of the place. Proceeding, I opened a swing door, drew aside a curtain and stood
within the theatre. Pity me, my grandchildren, pity me. Oh, if
you have hearts that feel—and I know you have—you will pity
your miserable grandfather. Of all the awful sights imprinted on
these eyes that day, relentlessly impressed upon a too-faithful
memory, I witnessed then the most horrible, the most gruesome,
the most ghostly and unutterably terrific of all. I stood upon the
floor of the theatre, close to the stage, within the portion of the
house then called "the stalls," and from that point I had a full and
instant view of the whole interior. The gas still burnt, and threw
a light upon the scene more brilliant than perhaps it had been on
the previous night; and the people—no, *not* the people, the
DEAD!—there under the glaring light they sat, they lay, they
hung over the benches, the galleries, the boxes, in one tremendous picture of catastrophe! Beside me were soft and delicate
women with their shimmering silks and dainty dresses, with
jewels sparkling on their necks and arms, with bouquets and fans
and other frivolous etcetera, still emanating the perfume and rich
odours of the toilette; and with them were men in their sombre
garments and starched courtliness, all huddled in their places in
every attitude of frantic woe. Behind them stretched the "pit,"
filled with its crowd of commoner folk, mingled and inextrica-
bly involved in a chaos of heads and limbs and bodies, writhed
and knotted together into one great mass of dead men, dead
women, and dead children, too. Overhead, tier above tier, rose
the galleries, loaded with a ghastly freight of occupants, some of

whose bodies hung forward across the front. And the orchestra and stage had also their grim array of horrors. The scenery was set to represent some ancient palace hall, and the stage was open to its furthest limit. Piled upon the boards in fantastic heaps were the bodies of numbers of ballet girls, whose spangled, thousand-hued and tinselled costumes, and all the gorgeous effects of spectacle and ballet, made infinitely more fearful that still and silent scene. Right in the centre and front of the stage there lay one corpse, still fair in death, with streaming hair and jewelled arms, with royal robes and diadem, the queen and sovereign of the pageant; and she—oh, mercy!—had fallen prone upon the footlights. The dull, low flames had scorched and burned some of her drapery, and a sickening smoke still rose from the spot where a once white and rounded bosom pressed down upon the jets, now charred and—oh, why was reason left me to remember these sights? I turned to hasten out once more into the only less terrible street, and as I moved I stumbled over the body of a man. He had passed for youthful, possibly, the night before, but death had lifted the mask that art had made, and I saw the wrinkled face beneath the cracking paint, the false teeth half ejected from the drawn lips in their last fearful gasp, the claw-like hands clutching desperately at the chair, and the whole false roundness of the form lost in a shrunken, huddled heap.

Sickened almost to death at the horrors before me, like a drunken man I reeled out into the street again.

What boots it to recall the long succession of frightful sights I witnessed by the way? All up the Strand bodies lay thick as on some battle-field, save that never battle-field was so grimly terrible as this. Here was a part of the town that had been thronged with pleasure-seekers and with those who catered for them, when the crisis came. Cabs, carriages, and omnibuses were numerous here, some overturned in the struggle of their horses, some grouped together or standing singly in all directions, but all silent and motionless, with dead horses fallen from their shafts, with dead men and dead women upon and within them. Oh, appalling and doleful memory, why cannot I fly the remembrance? And bodies of men, of women, and even of children, gaily-dressed and ragged intermixed, were piled upon the pavements. Yes, there they lay, the old, the young, the rich, the poor; of all ranks, and stations, and qualities, all huddled in one cold and hideous death; while open eyes, piteous faces, distorted limbs, and strange, unnatural attitudes, told the tremendous tale of that sudden midnight agony.

At length I reached our home; I entered the house and descended to the basement where we dwelt. Impatiently and fearfully I opened the door and passed into the sitting-room. Yes, there they were. The fire was cold and gray, but the cat lay curled upon the rug in her accustomed place. In the armchair sat my mother, and beside her, on a stool, my sister, just as they often loved to sit, with arms embracing each other. Was it my voice that broke the horrid stillness of the room—so hoarse, so changed? "Mother! sister! darlings!" No answer. Nearer I went, treading slowly and tremblingly. Again my hoarse accents jarred the heavy air as I knelt and took my mother's hand. "Mother! sister! awake!"

Ah! God of mercy! The horrid truth came home to me at last. Dead! dead!!

*   *   *   *   *   *

Children, I can write no more. I am shaken—unutterably shaken by these recollections. Much more I saw and knew, but, in pity's sake, press me not to tell you of it. And when you read elsewhere, or others tell you of THE DOOM of that GREAT CITY, think with tender sorrow of the awful load of memory that has so long been borne by YOUR GRANDFATHER.

> "The rich, the poor, one common bed
>   Shall find in the unhonour'd grave
> Where weeds shall crown alike the head
>   Of tyrant and of slave."
>   *Marvell*[30]

30. These lines were almost certainly not written by Andrew Marvell. John Clare records in his diary on June 23, 1825, that he "[w]rote to Mrs. Emmerson and sent a letter to 'Hone's Everyday Book,' with a poem which I fathered on Andrew Marvell." J. L. Cherry, *Life and Remains of John Clare, the "Northamptonshire Peasant Poet*," (London: Frederick Warne, 1873), 88. Hone published an eight-stanza poem, which concluded with these same lines. On November 13, 1841, *Chamber's Edinburgh Journal* republished them as part of the poem, "Remonstrance against Cruelty," and attributed it to Andrew Marvel[l] in its "Gems from the Old English Poets" series. Edwin Paxton Hood would later credit the poem to Marvell in *Andrew Marvell: The Wit, Statesman, and Poet: His Life and Writings* (London: Patridge & Oakey, 1853). Twentieth-century collections do not attribute the poem or these lines to Marvell, including the authoritative Clarendon Press edition of *The Poems and Letters of Andrew Marvell* (Oxford: Clarendon Press, 1971). These lines conclude John Clare's poem "Death," first published in *Midsummer Cushion* (1978), edited by Anne Tibble, which collected many poems that Clare had wanted to publish in 1832.

NINETEENTH-CENTURY WRITING ON CLIMATE CHANGE

Nineteenth-century thinkers such as Charles Lyell and William Buckland established various concepts that remain foundational to our notion of the Anthropocene, including early understandings of climate change, paleontology, and the age of the Earth. George Perkins Marsh's *Man and Nature: Or, Physical Geography as Modified by Human Action* (1864) contributed to numerous discussions about the consequences of human actions on the environment and is often credited with popularizing the modern conservation movement. Our first appendix builds upon these thinkers to highlight emergent understandings of weather as both a scientific and popular phenomenon. Louis Agassiz, who was strongly influenced by Buckland and Lyell, developed a theory of an ice age and discussed the recession of glaciers engendered by rising temperatures. The excerpt from David Ansted and

Robert Drummond's essay "Weather" (1860) may suggest the influence of pioneering climate scientist Eunice Newton Foote, whose experiments illustrated how sunlight increased levels of carbon dioxide in the air, absorbing heat and altering the atmosphere.[1] The article also demonstrates the evolution of the study of weather as a serious occupation, deserving of scientific and public attention. We also include Richard Jefferies's fictional treatment "The Great Snow" (c. 1876), an unfinished story not published until the middle of the twentieth century, in which he demonstrates how this emergent scientific thought shaped the literary imagination and popular fears about climate emergencies. Our final entry, from Swedish scientist Svante Arrhenius, provides an early model of the greenhouse effect, in which he links increased levels of carbon dioxide with increased air temperatures.

1. DAVID ANSTED AND ROBERT DRUMMOND, FROM "WEATHER," *CORNHILL MAGAZINE* 2, NO. 11 (NOVEMBER 1860): 565–79

The state of the weather at any time depends so much on the state of the atmosphere, that whatever influences that gaseous envelope of the earth necessarily produces a result which is universal or local according to the nature of the influence. At an elevation of some 20,000 feet above the sea, the winds are far more regular and uniform than we are accustomed to, and there appear to be

---

1. See specifically Eunice Newton Foote, "Circumstances Affecting the Heat of the Sun's Rays," *American Journal of Science and Arts* 22 (1856): 382–83.

certain levels at which very distinct conditions generally prevail. Below these levels the ordinary estimate of the wind, as the very emblem of change, may be correct enough; but above, when a change in the temperature or direction of the air takes place, it exercises a wide influence; and as these winds are chiefly produced by the combined motions of the earth and moon, and the effects of the sun's rays near the equator, there cannot be a doubt that lunar influence and lunar atmospheric tides exercise a very distinct and essential influence on the weather. The same causes which produce the great tide on the ocean, produce an atmospheric tide following the moon—a bulging out of the whole mass of the air which cannot but affect the barometer, and to which, combined with the corresponding solar tide, we must attribute many of its more regular and periodic changes. It seems certain that the reflected rays from the moon also produce a result, sometimes in dissipating clouds, sometimes in affecting the fall of rain. The clouds disperse at the moon's rising more or less completely as the moon is nearer the full, this influence commencing about four days after new, and terminating about ten days after full.

But it is chiefly to the sun, that great central and dominating body of our system, that we must refer if we would trace the ultimate causes of weather.[2] The sun is believed to possess a central, and probably a dark and solid nucleus, far smaller than the body we see. Outside this nucleus are three distinct atmospheres, the innermost a transparent elastic fluid surrounding the dark body of the sun just as our own atmosphere envelops the earth.

2. See Foote, "Circumstances Affecting the Heat," 383.

Beyond this first atmosphere appears a second, enclosing it and consisting of vast clouds of phosphoric light, the result of gaseous combustion of the most intense kind. These clouds—if we may so call that most intense brightness, placed before whose rays as they reach us the whitest and purest artificial lights seen close at hand are dark shadows—are very irregular in form and magnitude, constantly in motion with an almost inconceivable rapidity, and subject to a periodic covering of groups of dark spots and occasional bright lines and markings.

*   *   *

The study of the weather, then, leads to the consideration of some of the highest problems and most remarkable speculations of physical astronomy, and connects itself directly with investigations concerning light, heat, and the various forms of electrical action. Like all honest inquiries into natural phenomena, it commences with observation and experiment of a simple and homely kind. It requires that a large number of facts should be recorded; it carries its inquiries through many departments of knowledge, apparently little related to each other; and it lands the inquirer at last on a far higher level than he originally anticipated. He who sets himself to record weather and draw deductions from his observations, is no trifler, and his labour is not light. He must not only daily, at the same hour, record the result of his observations; he must make the necessary corrections, and bring his work into such a state as to compare it with what others have done elsewhere; he must himself make the comparison of his own with other observations, and with his own observations of former years; he must watch the course of vegetation and the habit of animals, and must notice carefully all the particulars of every meteoric appearance; he must, if living on an island, estimate the influence of winds and ocean currents, not only of his own shores, but a thousand miles away from his place of observation; he must estimate the influence of the mountains, plains, and valleys of the adjacent continent; he must inquire concerning the snow and frost on the remote and scarcely inhabited shores of the polar lands, and the ice set free from those lands, and floating on the broad ocean; he must ever be ready to accept and act upon the slightest hint thrown out by nature or by his fellow observer; he must hold his knowledge firmly, and his opinions, prejudices, and mere impressions, very loosely;—in a word, he must be patient and persevering, always ready to receive and record facts, and always cautious in deducing or admitting theories.

2. LOUIS AGASSIZ, FROM "THE FORMATION OF GLACIERS," *ATLANTIC MONTHLY: A MAGAZINE OF LITERATURE, ART, AND POLITICS* 12 (NOVEMBER 1863): 568–76

We have as yet no clue to the source of this great and sudden change of climate.[3] Various suggestions have been made,—among

---

3. In 1837, Agassiz proposed a hypothesis of a planetary ice age to the Helvetic Society. After completing a tour of the British Isles and visiting Scotland with Buckland in 1840, he became convinced that his theory of an ice was true.

others, that formerly the inclination of the earth's axis was greater, or that a submersion of the continents under water might have produced a decided increase of cold; but none of these explanations are satisfactory, and science has yet to find any cause which accounts for all the phenomena connected with it. It seems, however, unquestionable that since the opening of the Tertiary age a cosmic summer and winter have succeeded each other, during which a Tropical heat and an Arctic cold have alternately prevailed over a great portion of the globe. In the so-called drift (a superficial deposit subsequent to the Tertiaries, of the origin of which I shall speak presently) there are found far to the south of their present abode the remains of animals whose home now is in the Arctics or the coldest parts of the Temperate Zones. Among them are the Musk-Ox, the Reindeer, the Walrus, the Seal, and many kinds of Shells characteristic of the Arctic regions. The northernmost part of Norway and Sweden is at this day the southern limit of the Reindeer in Europe; but their fossil remains are found in large quantities in the drift about the neighborhood of Paris, where their presence would, of course, indicate a climate similar to the one now prevailing in Northern Scandinavia. Side by side with the remains of the Reindeer are found those of the European Marmot, whose present home is in the mountains, about six thousand feet above the level of the sea. The occurrence of these animals in the superficial deposits of the plains of Central Europe, one of which is now confined to the high North, and the other to mountain-heights, certainly indicates an entire change of climatic conditions since the time of their existence. European Shells now confined to the Northern Ocean are found as fossils in Italy,—showing, that, while the present Arctic climate prevailed in the Temperate Zone, that of the Temperate Zone extended much farther south to the regions we now call sub-tropical. In America there is abundant evidence of the same kind; throughout the recent marine deposits of the Temperate Zone, covering the low lands above tide-water on this continent, are found fossil Shells whose present home is on the shores of Greenland. It is not only in the Northern hemisphere that these remains occur, but in Africa and in South America, wherever there has been an opportunity for investigation, the drift is found to contain the traces of animals whose presence indicates a climate many degrees colder than that now prevailing there.

But these organic remains are not the only evidence of the geological winter. There are a number of phenomena indicating that during this period two vast caps of ice stretched from the Northern pole southward and from the Southern pole northward, extending in each case far toward the Equator,—and that icefields, such as now spread over the Arctics, covered a great part of the Temperate Zones, while the line of perpetual ice and snow in the tropical mountain-ranges descended far below its present limits. As the explanation of these facts has been drawn from the study of glacial action, I shall devote this and subsequent articles to some account of glaciers and of the phenomena connected with them.

3. RICHARD JEFFERIES, FROM "THE GREAT SNOW" (C.1876)

Much difficulty was experienced in locomotion.[4] Trains were delayed but there was no interruption of the service, for the wind being still, there was no drift. All day and night of the 17th, 18th, 19th, and 20th the snow came steadily down, and on the 21st, despite all efforts to clear it, was 27 inches deep. Traffic in the streets was now suspended, and the steamers ceased to ply, partly from want of passengers, and partly because of the dangerous obscurity. Most of the lines were blocked, and on the 22nd when the snow had an even depth of 33 inches, not a train reached London. Business was at an end. Till now the snow had been treated as a good joke by the populace who pelted each other in high spirits at their holiday, but when the trains ceased to arrive a species of desponding stupor seemed to fall upon them. The 23rd was a windy day, the breeze increasing from the east, till in the evening it blew almost a hurricane. The grains of frozen snow lifted up and driven by the wind rushed up the streets like pellets from a gun. The narrow portals of Temple Bar were impassable, so vehement was the blast, and those who attempted to get through describe the hard snow as cutting the skin of their faces in a painful manner. This gale drifted the snow in huge mounds.

4. Jefferies's story was not published until Samuel Looker included it in his edition of uncollected works, *Beauty Is Immortal* (1948). Looker is responsible for the title "The Great Snow" and speculates that it was probably a sketch intended for *After London*. The manuscript of "The Great Snow" is available at the British Library (MS 58815).

On the morning of 24th the western side of Trafalgar Square was 18 feet deep in snow, the entrance to the Haymarket was blocked up, and Regent Street near the Quadrant was buried under more than 20 feet. The Thames Embankment was quite clear—the wind having an uninterrupted sweep up it—but the Houses of Parliament formed a dam across the stream of snow and against the eastern side there rose a mound at least 27 feet high. The fleet of merchantmen at the mouth of the Thames were driven on shore, and the whole northern and eastern coasts were strewn with wreckage. Many of these incidents were not ascertained till long afterwards, for the telegraph posts were blown down, the wires snapped, and all communication at an end. The bitter wind lasted five days, and is described as causing an insupportable cold which neither walls, nor curtains, nor roaring fires could overcome. It penetrated through everything.

*   *   *

On the 29th the gale moderated, but meantime snow had fallen unceasingly, and it had now reached an uniform depth of ten feet. With slight variations it continued at this depth but the drifts of course were of enormous height. The National Gallery was wholly hidden under a mound of snow. The dome of St. Paul's was alone visible, rising up like the roof of a huge Esquimoux hut. The great gilt cross on the top had been torn off by the violence of the wind. An intense frost set in, but the sky remained covered with a leaden pall of cloud, and the sun was invisible. All round the coasts there was an impenetrable wall of fog, and eight or ten icebergs are recorded to have come ashore.

A berg of immense size, after beating and grinding for days against Portland breakwater, at last worked its way into the harbour, and grounded. Another got up the Solent, and two white bears swam to land from it. A third iceberg of smaller size drifted along the south coast, and after sweeping away the Brighton piers, was carried out to sea again by the tide, and lost in the fog. Not a vessel could make her port; and none dared to put out to sea, so that communication with the Continent was totally interrupted. The depth of ten feet extended over the country. Railways, canals, roads, paths, fields, all were buried to that depth, and in places the drifts rose to one-hundred-and-fifty feet. Sheep and cattle were overwhelmed and perished by thousands. Those in stalls were in a few instances kept alive for a little while by the farmers, and herdsmen cutting holes down to them. The Thames was frozen, and on the 2nd March the ice was seven feet thick off the Tower. Below Gravesend the tides carried huge blocks up and down, dashing them against each other, and against the edge of the fixed ice with a most horrible noise. During the first days of this visitation a stuper fell upon the millions of London.

4. SVANTE ARRHENIUS, FROM "ON THE INFLUENCE OF CARBONIC ACID IN THE AIR UPON THE TEMPERATURE OF THE GROUND." *LONDON, EDINBURGH, AND DUBLIN PHILOSOPHICAL MAGAZINE AND JOURNAL OF SCIENCE* 41 (APRIL 1896): 237–76.

From geological researches the fact is well established that in Tertiary times there existed a vegetation and an animal life in the temperate and arctic zones that must have been conditioned by a much higher temperature than the present in the same regions. The temperature in the arctic zones appears to have exceeded the present temperature by about 8 or 9 degrees. To this genial time the ice age succeeded, and this was one or more times interrupted by interglacial periods with a climate of about the same character as the present, sometimes even milder. When the ice age had its greatest extent, the countries that now enjoy the highest civilization were covered with ice. This was the case with Ireland, Britain (except a small part in the south), Holland, Denmark, Sweden and Norway, Russia (to Kiev, Orel, and Nijni Novgorod), Germany and Austria (to the Harz, Erz-Gebirge, Dresden, and Cracow). At the same time an ice-cap from the Alps covered Switzerland, parts of France, Bavaria south of the Danube, the Tyrol, Styria, and other Austrian countries, and descended into the northern part of Italy. Simultaneously, too, North America was covered with ice on the west coast to the 47th parallel, on the east coast to the 40th, and in the central part to the 37th (confluence of the Mississippi and Ohio rivers). In the most different parts of the world, too, we have found traces of a great ice age, as in the Caucasus, Asia Minor, Syria, the Himalayas, India, Thian Shan, Altai, Atlas, on Mount Kenia and Kilimandjaro (both very near to the equator), in South Africa, Australia, New Zealand, Kerguelen, Falkland Islands, Patagonia and other parts of South America.[5]

5. Thian Shan: also known as the Tengri Tagh or Tengir-Too, a large series of mountain ranges in Central Asia; Altai: Russian republic in Southern

* * *

By measurements of the displacement of the snow-line we arrive at the result,—and this is very concordant for different places—that the temperature at that time must have been 4°–5° C. lower than at present. The last glaciation must have taken place in rather recent times, geologically speaking, so that the human race certainly had appeared at that period. Certain American geologists hold the opinion that since the close of the ice age only some 7[,]000 to 10,000 years have elapsed, but this most probably is greatly underestimated.

One may now ask, How much must the carbonic acid vary according to our figures, in order that the temperature should attain the same values as in the Tertiary and Ice ages respectively? A simple calculation shows that the temperature in the arctic regions would rise about 8° to 9° C., if the carbonic acid increased to 2·5 or 3 times its present value.[6]

* * *

Siberia and mountain range in Central and Eastern Asia at the intersection of Russia, China, Mongolia, and Kazakhstan; "Atlas": Mountain range in the Magherb in North Africa; Mount Kenia: Mount Kenya, the second highest mountain in Africa; Kilimandjaro: Mount Kilimanjaro, in Tanzania, the highest mountain in Africa; Kerguelen: The Kerguelen Islands, also known as the Desolation Islands, an island group in the sub-Antarctic region that make up one of the two exposed areas of the Kerguelen Plateau in the southern Indian Ocean.

6. Arrhenius attempts to determine if an increase of greenhouse gases could help explain the temperature variation between glacial and interglacial periods.

There is now an important question which should be answered, namely:—Is it probable that such great variations in the quantity of carbonic acid as our theory requires have occurred in relatively short geological times?[7] The answer to this question is given by Prof. [Arvid] Högbom.[8] As his memoir on this question may not be accessible to most readers of these pages, I have summed up and translated his utterances which are of most importance to our subject:—

* * *

"The following calculation is also very instructive for the appreciation of the relation between the quantity of carbonic acid in the air and the quantities that are transformed. The world's present production of coal reaches in round numbers 500 millions of tons per annum, or 1 ton per km.[2] of the earth's surface. Transformed into carbonic acid, this quantity would correspond to about a thousandth part of the carbonic acid in the atmosphere. It represents a layer of limestone of 0·003 millim. thickness over the whole globe, or 1·5 km^3 in cubic measure. This quantity of carbonic acid, which is supplied to the atmosphere chiefly by modern industry, may be regarded as completely compensating the quantity of carbonic acid that is consumed in the formation

7. carbonic acid: Arrhenius and Högbom refer to carbon dioxide as carbonic acid. Arrhenius does not directly attribute global warming to the burning of fossil fuels, but his paper is the one of the first to speculate on the impact of the role of carbon dioxide on the variation in atmospheric conditions.
8. Swedish geologist (1857–1940) credited with making the first estimates on carbon dioxide emissions into the atmosphere from fossil fuel combustion.

of limestone (or other mineral carbonates) by the weathering or decomposition of silicates. From the determination of the amounts of dissolved substances, especially carbonates, in a number of rivers in different countries and climates, and of the quantity of water flowing in these rivers and of their drainage-surface compared with the land-surface of the globe, it is estimated that the quantities of dissolved carbonates that are supplied to the ocean in the course of a year reach at most the bulk of $3km^3$."

GLOBAL PERSPECTIVES ON THE CITY

Spanning over a century, the following selections offer a series of perspectives on the city as a civilizing project, a contact zone between colonial subjects, and an imaginative geography that generates dreams of more sustainable futures. Mirza Salih Shirazi offers an early outsider's perspective on the cultural practices of London city parks during his travels as a representative of the Iranian court on an educational trip across England. Mary Seacole describes a very different encounter on the streets of London as a colonial subject who long dreamed of traveling to the capital as a child—only to recollect her experience of the city later in life as "sometimes a rather chequered one." Rudyard Kipling presents a portrait of the city of Lahore as it has grown within its walls under British colonialism, leading to crowded conditions that dehumanize its inhabitants and blur the line between the living and the dead. An excerpt from Rokeya Sakhawat Hossain's *Sultana's Dream* describes a walking tour of a city of the future where the urban concerns of crowding, famine, pollution, and labor are effectively solved through technological innovations produced by women-led universities. Finally, Gandhi's interview with the *News Chronicle* provides an early twentieth-century comparative perspective on experiences of economic inequality between the city of London and the cities of India.

1. MIRZA SALIH SHIRAZI, FROM *THE COLLECTED JOURNEYS OF MIRZA SALIH SHIRAZI* (1815). PASSAGE TRANSLATED BY NILE GREEN.

In London, there are four "parks" . . . That is to say, public gardens . . . One park is Hyde Park; another is St. James's Park; another is Green Park; and another is Regent's Park.[1] In each of them, the people of London come there at one o'clock in the afternoon to spend time strolling around and conversing. Men and women, who might be family or friends, lock hands as they stroll. Those who have their own carriages go there in their carriages; other people ride horses. They stay there, ambling around, till it gets dark. But it is the custom there that no-one at all speaks loudly. If a blind person went there, he would imagine that none of them could speak or that speaking had been banned there!

---

1. Mirza Salih Shirazi was a nineteenth-century Iranian newspaper reporter and intellectual. The name "Mirza Salih Shirazi" is transliterated from Farsi and as a result is also referenced as "Mirza Saleh Shirazi" in some English language sources. This travelogue is discussed at length in Nile Green's *For the Love of Strangers: What Six Muslim Students Learned in Jane Austen's London* (Princeton: Princeton University Press, 2016), 284.

2. MARY SEACOLE, FROM *WONDERFUL ADVENTURES OF MRS. SEACOLE IN MANY LANDS* (1857)

As I grew into womanhood, I began to indulge that longing to travel which will never leave me while I have health and vigour. I was never weary of tracing upon an old map the route to England; and never followed with my gaze the stately ships homeward bound without longing to be in them, and see the blue hills of Jamaica fade into the distance. At that time it seemed most improbable that these girlish wishes should be gratified; but circumstances, which I need not explain, enabled me to accompany some relatives to England while I was yet a very young woman.

I shall never forget my first impressions of London. Of course, I am not going to bore the reader with them; but they are as vivid now as though the year 18—(I had very nearly let my age slip then) had not been long ago numbered with the past. Strangely enough, some of the most vivid of my recollections are the efforts of the London street-boys to poke fun at my and my companion's complexion. I am only a little brown—a few shades duskier than the brunettes whom you all admire so much; but my companion was very dark, and a fair (if I can apply the term to her) subject for their rude wit. She was hot-tempered, poor thing! and as there were no policemen to awe the boys and turn our servants' heads in those days, our progress through the London streets was sometimes a rather chequered one.

3. RUDYARD KIPLING, FROM "THE CITY OF DREADFUL NIGHT" (1885)

The dense wet heat that hung over the face of land, like a blanket, prevented all hope of sleep in the first instance.[2] The cicalas helped the heat; and the yelling jackals the cicalas.[3] It was impossible to sit still in the dark, empty, echoing house and watch the punkah beat the dead air.[4] So, at ten o'clock of the night, I set my walking-stick on end in the middle of the garden, and waited to see how it would fall. It pointed directly down the moonlit road that leads to the City of Dreadful Night. The sound of its fall disturbed a hare. She limped from her form and ran across to a disused Mahomedan burial-ground, where the jawless skulls and rough-butted shank-bones, heartlessly exposed by the July rains, glimmered like mother o' pearl on the rain-channelled soil. The heated air and the heavy earth had driven the very dead upward for coolness' sake. The hare limped on; snuffed curiously at a fragment of a smoke-stained lamp-shard, and died out, in the shadow of a clump of tamarisk trees.[5]

2. First published in the *Civil and Military Gazette* in 1885, but is later collected in *Life's Handicap: Being Stories Of Mine Own People* (London: Macmillan, 1891) 321–28.

3. Alternative name for "cicada," large insects that produce loud, droning sounds.

4. punkah: large cloth fan suspended from the ceiling and moved back and forth by pulling on a cord.

5. In Lahore, evergreen trees with slender branches and many small leaves. Known for growing in saline soils.

The mat-weaver's hut under the lee of the Hindu temple was full of sleeping men who lay like sheeted corpses. Overhead blazed the unwinking eye of the Moon. Darkness gives at least a false impression of coolness. It was hard not to believe that the flood of light from above was warm. Not so hot as the Sun, but still sickly warm, and heating the heavy air beyond what was our due. Straight as a bar of polished steel ran the road to the City of Dreadful Night; and on either side of the road lay corpses disposed on beds in fantastic attitudes—one hundred and seventy bodies of men. Some shrouded all in white with bound-up mouths; some naked and black as ebony in the strong light; and one—that lay face upwards with dropped jaw, far away from the others—silvery white and ashen gray.

'A leper asleep; and the remainder wearied coolies, servants, small shopkeepers, and drivers from the hack-stand hard by.[6] The scene—a main approach to Lahore city, and the night a warm one in August.' This was all that there was to be seen; but by no means all that one could see. The witchery of the moon-light was everywhere; and the world was horribly changed. The long line of the naked dead, flanked by the rigid silver statue, was not pleasant to look upon. It was made up of men alone. Were the womenkind, then, forced to sleep in the shelter of the stifling mud-huts as best they might? The fretful wail of a child from a low mud-roof answered the question. Where the children are the mothers must be also to look after them. They need care on these

6. coolies: laborers.

sweltering nights. A black little bullethead peeped over the coping, and a thin—a painfully thin—brown leg was slid over on to the gutter pipe. There was a sharp clink of glass bracelets; a woman's arm showed for an instant above the parapet, twined itself round the lean little neck, and the child was dragged back, protesting, to the shelter of the bedstead. His thin, high-pitched shriek died out in the thick air almost as soon as it was raised; for even the children of the soil found it too hot to weep.

More corpses; more stretches of moonlit, white road; a string of sleeping camels at rest by the wayside; a vision of scudding jackals; ekka-ponies asleep[7]—the harness still on their backs, and the brass-studded country carts, winking in the moonlight— and again more corpses. Wherever a grain cart atilt, a tree trunk, a sawn log, a couple of bamboos and a few handfuls of thatch cast a shadow, the ground is covered with them. They lie—some face downwards, arms folded, in the dust; some with clasped hands flung up above their heads; some curled up dog-wise; some thrown like limp gunny-bags over the side of the grain carts; and some bowed with their brows on their knees in the full glare of the Moon. It would be a comfort if they were only given to snoring; but they are not, and the likeness to corpses is unbroken in all respects save one. The lean dogs snuff at them and turn away. Here and there a tiny child lies on his father's bedstead, and a protecting arm is thrown round it in every instance. But, for the most part, the children sleep with

7. ekka: a single-horse carriage.

their mothers on the housetops. Yellow-skinned white-toothed pariahs are not to be trusted within reach of brown bodies.[8]

A stifling hot blast from the mouth of the Delhi Gate nearly ends my resolution of entering the City of Dreadful Night at this hour. It is a compound of all evil savours, animal and vegetable, that a walled city can brew in a day and a night. The temperature within the motionless groves of plantain and orange-trees outside the city walls seems chilly by comparison. Heaven help all sick persons and young children within the city to-night!

4. ROKEYA SAKHAWAT HOSSAIN, FROM *SULTANA'S DREAM* (1905)

"Now, dear Sultana, will you sit here or come to my parlour?" she asked me.[9]

"Your kitchen is not inferior to a queen's boudoir!" I replied with a pleasant smile, "but we must leave it now; for the gentlemen may be cursing me for keeping them away from their duties in the kitchen so long." We both laughed heartily.

"How my friends at home will be amused and amazed, when I go back and tell them that in the far-off Lady-land, ladies rule

8. Pariah refers to a common dog breed in India, often used to refer to any stray dog; it is originally a Tamil word describing members of a low caste in Southern India.

9. Originally published in Madras in the *Indian Ladies' Magazine* 5, no. 3 (September 1905): 82–86. Our excerpt comes from the reprint in Abdul Kadir ed. *Rokeya Rachanabali* (Dhaka: Bangla Academy, 1971), 461–74.

over the country and control all social matters, while gentlemen are kept in the Murdanas to mind babies, to cook and to do all sorts of domestic work; and that cooking is so easy a thing that it is simply a pleasure to cook!"[10]

"Yes, tell them about all that you see here."

"Please let me know, how you carry on land cultivation and how you plough the land and do other hard manual work."

"Our fields are tilled by means of electricity, which supplies motive power for other hard work as well and we employ it for our aerial conveyances too. We have no rail road nor any paved streets here."

"Therefore neither streets nor railway accidents occur here," said I.

"Do not you ever suffer from want of rainwater?" I asked.

"Never since the 'water balloon' has been set up. You see the big balloon and pipes attached thereto. By their aid we can draw as much rainwater as we require. Nor do we ever suffer from flood or thunderstorms. We are all very busy making nature yield as much as she can. We do not find time to quarrel with one another as we never sit idle. Our noble Queen is exceedingly fond of Botany; it is her ambition to convert the whole country into one grand garden."

"The idea is excellent. What is your chief food?"

"Fruits."

---

10. Murdana (often spelled "mardana") is a public part of the house reserved for men. Here, described satirically in respect to the "zenana," a private part of the house usually reserved for women.

"How do you keep your country cool in hot weather? We regard the rainfall in summer as a blessing from heaven."

"When the heat becomes unbearable, we sprinkle the ground with plentiful showers drawn from the artificial fountains. And in cold weather we keep our room warm with sun-heat."

*   *   *

"That is very good. I see purity itself reigns over your land. I should like to see the good Queen, who is so sagacious and far-sighted and who has made all these rules."

"All right," said Sister Sara.

Then she screwed a couple of seats onto a square piece of plank. To this plank she attached two smooth and well-polished balls. When I asked her what the balls were for, she said they were hydrogen balls and they were used to overcome the force of gravity.[11] The balls were of different capacities to be used according to the different weights desired to be overcome. She then fastened to the air-car two wing-like blades, which, she said, were worked by electricity. After we were comfortably seated she touched a knob and the blades began to whirl, moving faster and faster every moment. At first we were raised to the height of about six or seven feet and then off we flew. And before I could realize that we had commenced moving we reached the Garden of the Queen.

11. The choice of "hydrogen" here is both technologically and ecologically significant, as there is a nineteenth-century history of hydrogen-powered engines dating back as early as Isaac de Rivaz's hydrogen-powered engine. In 1863, Etienne Lenoir designed the "Hippomobile," an early car fueled by electrolyzing water and running hydrogen through its engine.

My friend lowered the air-car by reversing the action of the machine, and when the car touched the ground the machine was stopped and we got out.

5. MOHANDAS KARAMCHAND GANDHI, FROM "INTERVIEW TO 'THE NEWS CHRONICLE'"

LONDON,
[September 17,1931][12]

*   *   *

I love the East End, particularly the little urchins in the streets. They give me such friendly greetings. I have seen a tremendous change in social conditions since I was in London forty years ago. The poverty in London is nothing to what it is in India. I go down the streets here and I see outside each house a bottle of milk, and inside the door there is a strip of carpet, perhaps a piano in the sitting room.

In India several millions wear only a loin-cloth. That is why I wear a loin-cloth myself. They call me half-naked. I do it deliberately in order to identify myself with the poorest of the poor in India. What impresses me about London is that there is not the same glaring difference between rich and poor. As I drive down in my car to Bow every night, I have been noticing how gradual is

12. "The source does not mention the date. But the correspondent said Gandhiji gave him the interview 'yesterday'. If he was writing on the 18th, the interview probably took place on the 17th" [footnote from *Collected Works* edition].

the change from the riches of the West End to the poverty of the East End. It is perhaps not an exaggeration to say that the poor in London have as high a standard of living as the rich in India.

*   *   *

The News Chronicle, 19-9-1931[13]

---

13. Original date of publication of the interview [note in original].

THE LONDON FOG

Scholars of the Anthropocene have drawn attention to the history of the London fog as an example of how human actions upon a local environment have global effects. Hay's novella dramatizes a fantastic climatic event, but he was not alone in forecasting and imagining extraordinary circumstances associated with the London fog.[1] Francis Albert Rollo Russell's *London Fogs* (1880), published the same year as Hay's novella, provided foreboding descriptions of the atmosphere of the city and detailed descriptions of its dangers, including accounts of recent fatal events. We also include a selection from Robert Barr's "The Doom of London" (1892), a short story often compared with Hay's novella, and a brief excerpt from an article published in *The British Architect* (1880), in which the author highlights how burning coal has augmented the fogs of London. Our final entry is an image,

---

1. See also John Ruskin's *The Storm Cloud of the Nineteenth Century: Two Lectures Delivered at the London Institution. February 4th and 11th, 1884* (London: George Allen, 1884), in which Ruskin foreshadows numerous environmental concerns tied to London's atmospheric conditions.

"A London Fog" (1849), from *The Illustrated London News* that portrays the ambiguity, confusion, and dismay of the fog.

1. FRANCIS ALBERT ROLLO RUSSELL, FROM *LONDON FOGS* (1880)

In winter more than a million chimneys breathe forth simultaneously smoke, soot, sulphurous acid, vapour of water, and carbonic acid gas, and the whole town fumes like a vast crater, at the bottom of which its unhappy citizens must creep and live as best they can. If a moderate breeze blows, the products of combustion are removed to other parts of the atmosphere as fast as they are formed, and no dark fog can exist. But when the air is nearly or completely calm, the case is different. In winter the earth does not become sufficiently warmed by the sun to cause the air near its surface to rise, and the lowest atmospheric strata gain little heat even in the open country. When a substance not susceptible of evaporation obscures the low-lying fog-cloud even before sunrise, the cloud cannot gain warmth sufficient to dissipate it if the conditions which produced the fog are maintained. These conditions are, usually, the mixture of opposite winds and a clear sky above the fog-bank. Of what does a London fog consist? First, of a multitude of watery particles, such as make up a common fog; secondly, of a vast number of flakes of soot of various sizes; thirdly, of smoke proper, or minute particles of carbon; and fourthly, possibly, of smoke or carbon particles joined to the watery particles of the fog. Smoke and soot are not soluble or easily mixed in water, and it is therefore not likely that the particles of smoke actually dissolve in the water particles. There is repulsion, not adhesion, between the two substances, and a London fog is well accounted for by the accumulation of smoke alone, which any one can see to be dense and persistent enough when it comes straight from the grate into his room, where there is no condensed vapour of water. The fact is, that the white fog-cloud or stratus prevents the ascent and dissipation of the smoke which is ejected into it in the morning, and then the accumulated smoke mass in its turn resists the rays of the sun, and so prevents the evaporation of the natural fog.

* * *

The fog of Christmas Day, 1879, was attended with nocturnal darkness in London. In the country it was remarkably thick throughout the day.[2]

Some of the great fogs of the end of January and beginning of February, 1880, were uncommon in their character and development. On the 27th of January there was a sudden great increase in the intensity of the frost, almost absolute calm prevailed, and the easterly current gave way on the ground to a westerly air, with which it became intimately mixed. The east wind apparently continued at a moderate elevation. In many parts of London the fog was exceedingly dark, being mixed with a great volume of smoke, and the sun was invisible. At Hammersmith, at midday, the sun was just visible, at Richmond shining

2. See Bill Luckin, "'The Heart and Home of Horror,'" *Social History* 28, no. 1 (January 2003): 31–48.

dimly, and at Willesden very brightly.[3] The fog was not inconveniently thick outside London till the evening, when it greatly increased in density. At Richmond, at 2.45 P.M., the thermometer stood at 22, an extremely low temperature. More or less fog occurred here and there on the following days, and the sky remained clear above it. On the 30th and 31st an exceedingly light lower current from the south moved over southern England, greatly augmenting the temperature. Radiation, however, was not arrested by clouds, and the ground being chilled to a temperature much below the freezing-point by the previous severe frosts, did not thaw even when the thermometer stood at 45 in the open air. Thus, in certain localities, especially those least exposed to sunshine, very dense clouds were formed upon the ground by the reduction of the temperature of this slow warm current below the dew-point. On the 31st, at 10 A.M., a ground fog of extraordinary density, little discoloured by smoke, lay over parts of the south-western district of London. I measured the distance at which objects became visible, and found it to be four and a half yards. In some places the fog did not extend as high as the tops of the houses, and the smoke thus escaped into the upper air. In central London, great darkness accompanied the fog during the morning. This fog differed from most others in being entirely due to the chilling of a single atmospheric current by contact with the earth; and for this reason it extended in its intensity only a few feet above the ground. The day was

3. Hammersmith is a West London district. Richmond is a town in south-western London. Willesden is an area of northwestern London.

extremely fine in some of the suburbs. In the evening, with a rapid fall of temperature, the fog returned and caused the greatest difficulty to locomotion. On the 1st of February the atmosphere was less foggy in most districts, but again became almost impenetrable for traffic in the early morning of the 2nd. On the 4th the fog was again exceedingly thick. The fog had thus lasted eight days, on and off, with very great intensity. They were remarkable for their local character, the shady side of a square being several times plunged in a dense mist, while the opposite side rejoiced in sunshine; one end of Piccadilly in thick darkness, while the other remained bright and clear.[4]

* * *

Beyond these bodily hurts, the presence of an overshadowing cloud of smoke produces moral evils which at least deserve some consideration. The population which has hitherto made no serious effort to rid itself of the pollution with which it contaminates the vital breath of heaven suffers seriously for its neglect. They lose, in the first place, that glorious and almost universal privilege of looking upon the clear azure above them, a clear-setting sun or clear-rising moon, the magnificent cloud-castles of summer, the delicate hues and forms of clouds, and the crisp brilliancy of every fine winter morning. They lose, too, all distant prospects, urban or rural, and the pleasant variations of cloud-shadows which delight us in the views of great continental cities, which are not

4. Piccadilly is a central road in the City of Westminster, London between Hyde Park and Piccadilly Circus.

blurred or blotted out by smoke. These things are sermons from nature which humanity has need of. London is indeed hideous to look at, but would be less hideous without its smoke. What is the meaning of the expression, "Going to the country for fresh air," but that Londoners, of whom there are three millions, spend the greater part of their existence in foul air, surely a vast deprivation of a natural blessing? Many a life has been saved by timely removal to country pursuits. It is no joke to those who cannot leave their occupation. Air is to man more than water is to fish; he not only moves in it, but breathes it and lives upon it, and contaminated air deprived of its ozone fails duly to refresh him. If we examine the conditions of various trades, we find that those which are most unwholesome to the body tend also to crush out the wholesome buoyancy of the mind.

2. ROBERT BARR, FROM "THE DOOM OF LONDON" (1892)

London at the end of the 19th century consumed vast quantities of a soft bituminous coal for the purpose of heating rooms and of preparing food. In the morning and during the day, clouds of black smoke were poured forth from thousands of chimneys. When a mass of white vapour arose in the night these clouds of smoke fell upon the fog, pressing it down, filtering slowly through it, and adding to its density. The sun would have absorbed the fog but for the layer of smoke that lay thick above the vapour and prevented its rays reaching it. Once this condition of things prevailed, nothing could clear London but a breeze of wind from any direction. London frequently had a seven days' fog, and sometimes a seven days' calm, but these two conditions never coincided until the last year of the last century. The coincidence, as everyone knows, meant death—death so wholesale that no war the earth has ever seen left such slaughter behind it. To understand the situation, one has only to imagine the fog as taking the place of the ashes at Pompeii, and the coal-smoke as being the lava that covered it. The result to the inhabitants in both cases was exactly the same.

* * *

It was on a Friday that the fog came down upon us. The weather was very fine up to the middle of November that autumn. The fog did not seem to have anything unusual about it. I have seen many worse fogs than that appeared to be. As day followed day, however, the atmosphere became denser and darker, caused, I suppose, by the increasing volume of coal-smoke poured out upon it. The peculiarity about those seven days was the intense stillness of the air. We were, although we did not know it, under an air-proof canopy, and were slowly but surely exhausting the life-giving oxygen around us, and replacing it by poisonous carbonic acid gas. Scientific men have since showed that a simple mathematical calculation might have told us exactly when the last atom of oxygen would have been consumed; but it is easy to be wise after the event. The body of the greatest mathematician in England was found in the Strand. He came that morning from Cambridge. During the fog there was always a marked increase in the death rate, and on this occasion the increase was no greater than usual until the sixth day. The newspapers on the morning of the seventh were full of startling statistics, but at the time of going to press the full significance of the alarming figures was not realised. The editorials of the morning papers on the seventh day contained no warning of the calamity that was so speedily to follow their appearance. I lived then at Ealing, a Western suburb of London, and came every morning to Cannon Street by a certain train. I had up to the sixth day experienced no inconvenience from the fog, and this was largely due, I am convinced, to the unnoticed operations of the American machine.[5] On the fifth and sixth days Sir John did not come to the City, but he was in his office on the seventh. The door between his room and mine was closed. Shortly after ten o'clock I heard a cry in his room, followed by a heavy fall. I opened the door, and saw Sir John lying face downwards on the floor. Hastening towards him, I felt for the first time the deadly effect of the deoxygenised atmosphere, and before I reached him I fell first on one knee and then headlong. I realised that my senses were leaving me, and instinctively crawled back to my own room, where the oppression was at once lifted, and I stood again upon my feet, gasping. I closed the door of Sir John's room, thinking it filled with poisonous fumes, as,

5. Robert Barr, "The Doom of London," *Idler: An Illustrated Magazine* 2 (1892): 401. The narrator meets the referenced American inventor while working as a clerk at the house of Fulton, Brixton & Co. in Cannon Street. The inventor offers an oxygen machine "that would revolutionise life in London.... The machine, which he had in a small handbag with him, was of white metal, and it was so constructed that by turning an index it gave out greater or less volumes of oxygen gas."

indeed, it was. I called loudly for help, but there was no answer. On opening the door to the main office I met again what I thought was the noxious vapor. Speedily as I closed the door, I was impressed by the intense silence of the usually busy office, and saw that some of the clerks were motionless on the floor, and others sat with their heads on their desks as if asleep. Even at this awful moment I did not realise that what I saw was common to all London, and not, as I imagined, a local disaster, caused by the breaking of some carboys in our cellar. (It was filled with chemicals of every kind, of whose properties I was ignorant, dealing as I did with the accountant, and not the scientific side of our business.) I opened the only window in my room, and again shouted for help. The street was silent and dark in the ominously still fog, and what now froze me with horror was meeting the same deadly, stifling atmosphere that was in the rooms. In falling I brought down the window, and shut out the poisonous air. Again I revived, and slowly the true state of things began to dawn upon me. I was in an oasis of oxygen. I at once surmised that the machine on my shelf was responsible for the existence of this oasis in a vast desert of deadly gas. I took down the American's machine, fearful in moving it that I might stop its working. Taking the mouthpiece between my lips I again entered Sir John's room, this time without feeling any ill effects. My poor master was long beyond human help. There was evidently no one alive in the building except myself. Out in the street all was silent and dark. The gas was extinguished, but here and there in shops the incandescent lights were still weirdly burning, depending, as they did, on accumulators, and not on direct engine power. I turned automatically towards Cannon Street Station, knowing my way to it even if blindfolded, stumbling over bodies prone on the pavement, and in crossing the street I ran against a motionless 'bus, spectral in the fog, with dead horses lying in front, and their reins dangling from the nerveless hand of a dead driver. The ghostlike passengers, equally silent, sat bolt upright, or hung over the edge-boards in attitudes horribly grotesque.

3. FROM "METROPOLITAN ATMOSPHERIC POLLUTION." *BRITISH ARCHITECT* 14, NO. 3 (16 JULY 1880): 25–26.

The oppressive character of London air was probably largely due to the enormous consumption of [coal].

The quantity of coal estimated to be consumed annually in London was about 5,000,000 tons, and London air contained about 19 grains of sulphurous acid in a cubic yard of air. The darkness which prevailed in London last winter was to a large extent due to the smoke-polluted air. Very slight efforts had been made in the direction of purifying the air of towns from smoke. This was a matter which must depend rather upon the efforts of the individual householder than upon the centralised action of the local authorities. Under the present system of warming houses, the colder and more raw the weather is, the greater must be the quantity of smoke and soot driven into the atmosphere of our towns. The ordinary open fire consumed a far greater amount of fuel than was necessary for warmth, and almost all ranges used in kitchens consumed far more coal than was required for mere purposes of cooking. Captain Galton then dwelt at length upon various methods of economising fuel and storing heat,[6] with the view of diminishing the amount of coal consumed in domestic fires, which would keep the air of London in a far purer condition than it was at present. He contrasted the recently-erected model lodging-houses with the habitations in St. Giles's, which required to be reconstructed on sanitary principles.

4. "A LONDON FOG," *ILLUSTRATED LONDON NEWS*, DECEMBER 22, 1849.

Figure 3. "A London Fog." *Illustrated London News*, December 22, 1849. Michelle Bridges/Alamy Stock Photo.

6. Douglas Galton (1822–1899) was a British engineer and captain of the Royal Engineers. He became a member of the Royal Commission of Railways and served as Directory of Public Works and Buildings from 1869–1875. He was cousin to the eugenicist Francis Galton and collaborated extensively with Florence Nightingale.

VICTORIAN PUBLIC HEALTH

These nineteenth- and early twentieth-century selections document emergent understandings of how the environments in which people live affect their health, both at the individual and social scale. Edwin Chadwick's *Report on the Sanitary Condition of the Labouring Population of Great Britain* (1842) documents the living conditions of the working class in small towns as well as cities and points to failures in urban design and waste removal as a source of "epidemic" and premature death. The excerpt from Florence Nightingale's *Notes on Nursing for the Labouring Classes* (1861) builds on understandings of the social determinants of health, including the full range of environmental conditions that influence people's thriving. Nightingale empowers and indicts readers in her descriptions of disease prevention made possible through interventions in single-family dwelling construction and sanitation. Informed by Muscular Christianity, Charles Kingsley's "The Science of Health" (1874) frames individual choices in diet and exercise as methods of preventive medicine. He aligns the body with the "laws of Nature . . . the good will of God expressed in facts" and references concerns Nightingale and others raise about social and racial "degeneration." Finally, an advertisement for Peps cough tablets depicts the figure of death amid fog and clouds that swirl above a city, strikingly rendering the environmental effects of pollution on the health of the city's inhabitants as they flee its threat.

1. EDWIN CHADWICK, FROM *REPORT ON THE SANITARY CONDITION OF THE LABOURING POPULATION OF GREAT BRITAIN* (1842)

After as careful an examination of the evidence collected as I have been enabled to make, I beg leave to recapitulate the chief conclusions which that evidence appears to me to establish.[1]

First, as to the extent and operation of the evils which are the subject of this inquiry:—

1. Chadwick began the inquiry in 1839 and published his initial report in 1842. It was completed and published at his own expense, becoming a best-selling publication produced by the Stationery Office. Chadwick convinced the Poor Law Board that an inquiry into sanitary conditions was necessary following a critical outbreak of typhus in 1838. This was the first British inquiry into public health in which physicians were employed to examine social and living conditions that might influence the population.

That the various forms of epidemic, endemic, and other disease caused, or aggravated, or propagated chiefly amongst the labouring classes by atmospheric impurities produced by decomposing animal and vegetable substances, by damp and filth, and close and overcrowded dwellings prevail amongst the population in every part of the kingdom, whether dwelling in separate houses, in rural villages, in small towns, in the larger towns—as they have been found to prevail in the lowest districts of the metropolis.

That such disease, wherever its attacks are frequent, is always found in connexion with the physical circumstances above specified, and that where those circumstances are removed by drainage, proper cleansing, better ventilation, and other means of diminishing atmospheric impurity, the frequency and intensity of such disease is abated; and where the removal of the noxious agencies appears to be complete, such disease almost entirely disappears.

That high prosperity in respect to employment and wages, and various and abundant food, have afforded to the labouring classes no exemptions from attacks of epidemic disease, which have been as frequent and as fatal in periods of commercial and manufacturing prosperity as in any others.

That the formation of all habits of cleanliness is obstructed by defective supplies of water.

That the annual loss of life from filth and bad ventilation are greater than the loss from death or wounds in any wars in which the country has been engaged in modern times.

That of the 43,000 cases of widowhood, and 112,000 cases of destitute orphanage relieved from the poor's rates in England and Wales alone, it appears that the greatest proportion of deaths of the heads of families occurred from the above specified and other removable causes; that their ages were under 45 years; that is to say, 13 years below the natural probabilities of life as shown by the experience of the whole population of Sweden.

That the public loss from the premature deaths of the heads of families is greater than can be represented by any enumeration of the pecuniary burdens consequent upon their sickness and death.

That, measuring the loss of working ability amongst large classes by the instances of gain, even from incomplete arrangements for the removal of noxious influences from places of work or from abodes, that this loss cannot be less than eight or ten years.

That the ravages of epidemics and other diseases do not diminish but tend to increase the pressure of population.

That in the districts where the mortality is greatest the births are not only sufficient to replace the numbers removed by death, but to add to the population.

That the younger population, bred up under noxious physical agencies, is inferior in physical organization and general health to a population preserved from the presence of such agencies.

That the population so exposed is less susceptible of moral influences, and the effects of education are more transient than with a healthy population.

That these adverse circumstances tend to produce an adult population short-lived, improvident, reckless, and intemperate, and with habitual avidity for sensual gratifications.

That these habits lead to the abandonment of all the conveniences and decencies of life, and especially lead to the overcrowding of their homes, which is destructive to the morality as well as the health of large classes of both sexes.

That defective town cleansing fosters habits of the most abject degradation and tends to the demoralization of large numbers of human beings, who subsist by means of what they find amidst the noxious filth accumulated in neglected streets and bye-places.

2. FLORENCE NIGHTINGALE, FROM *NOTES ON NURSING FOR THE LABOURING CLASSES* (1861)

THERE are five essential points in securing the health of houses:—[2]

1. Pure air.
2. Pure water.
3. Efficient drainage.
4. Cleanliness.
5. Light.

2. First published as a small volume in 1859 as *Notes on Nursing: What It Is and What It Is Not*, this text was expanded and republished many times with both abridgements and additions. For this excerpt, we referenced the 1861 edition that included a new subtitle.

Without these, no house can be healthy. And it will be unhealthy just in proportion as they are not.

1. To have pure air, your house must be so built as that the outer air shall find its way with ease to every corner of it. House builders hardly ever consider this. The object in building a house is to obtain the largest interest for the money, not to save doctor's bills to the tenants. But, if tenants should ever become so wise as to refuse to occupy unhealthily built houses, builders would speedily be brought to their senses. As it is, they build what pays best. And there are always people foolish enough to take the houses they build. And if in the course of time the families die off, as is so often the case, nobody ever thinks of blaming any but Providence for the result. Ill-informed people help to keep up the delusion, by laying the blame on "current contagions." Bad houses do for the healthy what bad hospitals do for the sick. Once insure that the air in a house is stagnant, and sickness is certain to follow.

*   *   *

2. Pure water is more general in houses than it used to be, thanks to the exertions of a few. Within the last few years, a large part of London was in the daily habit of using water polluted by the drainage of its sewers and water-closets. This has happily been remedied. But, in many parts of the country, well-water of a very impure kind is used for domestic purposes. And when epidemic disease shows itself, persons using such water are almost sure to suffer.

*   *   *

3. It would be curious to ascertain by inspection, how many houses said to be drained are really well drained. Many people would say, surely all or most of them. But many people have no idea in what good drainage consists. They think that a sewer in the street, and a pipe leading to it from the house is good drainage. All the while the sewer may be nothing but a place from which sickness and ill health are being poured into the house. No house with any untrapped unventilated drain pipe communicating immediately with an unventilated sewer, whether it be from water-closet, sink, or gully-grate, can ever be healthy. An untrapped sink may at any time spread fevers and other diseases among the inmates of a palace.

* * *

4. Without cleanliness, within and without your house, ventilation is comparatively useless. In certain foul districts poor people used to object to open their windows and doors because of the foul smells that came in. Rich people like to have their stables and dunghill near their houses. But does it ever occur to them that with many arrangements of this kind it would be safer to keep the windows shut than open? You cannot have the air of the house pure with dung heaps under the windows. These are common everywhere. And yet people are surprised that their children, brought up in "country air," suffer from children's diseases. If they studied nature's laws in the matter of children's health, they would not be so surprised.

* * *

5. A dark house is always an unhealthy house, always an ill-aired house, always a dirty house. Want of light stops growth, and promotes scrofula, rickets, &c., &c., among the children.[3]

People lose their health in a dark house, and if they get ill they cannot get well again in it. More will be said about this farther on.

* * *

It has been often stated that intermarriage, marrying cousins, is a fruitful source of family weakness and want of health; but is it considered that other habits descending from parents to off-spring, such, for instance, as intemperance, breathing foul air, living in gloomy unhealthy localities and the like, also tend to want of health?

In healthy "registration" districts, the mortality is low and the annual proportion of births is also low, but in unhealthy districts the mortality rises, while at the same time the proportion of births increases, showing that in such districts the circuit of life is shortened.[4]

3. scrofula: a type of tuberculosis infection caused by the same bacteria that causes pulmonary tuberculosis (TB). Scrofula is usually recognized by swelling in the neck due to infected lymph nodes. rickets: a childhood disease resulting in the softening of bones usually due to a prolonged deficiency of Vitamin D.
4. "Registration districts" are administrative regions that exist for the purposes of recording births, deaths, and marriages within a defined area.

3. CHARLES KINGSLEY, FROM "THE SCIENCE OF HEALTH" (1874)

The value of healthy habitations, of personal cleanliness, of pure air and pure water, of various kinds of food, according as each tends to make bone, fat, or muscle, provided only—provided only—that the food be unadulterated; the value of various kinds of clothing, and physical exercise, of a free and equal development of the brain-power, without undue overstrain in any one direction; in one word, the method of producing, as far as possible, the mentem sanam in corpore sano, and the wonderful and blessed effects of such obedience to those laws of nature, which are nothing but the good will of God expressed in facts—their wonderful and blessed tendency, I say, to eliminate the germs of hereditary disease, and to actually regenerate the human system—all this is known; known as fully and clearly as any human knowledge need be known; it is written in dozens of popular books and pamphlets.[5] And why should this divine voice, which cries to man, tending to sink into effeminate barbarism through his own hasty and partial civilisation,—"It is not too late. For your bodies, as for your spirits, there is an upward,

5. The essay was published in *Health and Education* in 1874; Kingsley notes that it developed from a lecture on "physical education" given at the Midland Institute, Birmingham, in 1872. "corpore sano": Allusion to a line from Roman poet Juvenal, *mens sana in corpore sano*, "healthy mind in a healthy body." Kingsley favors the accusative case in his use of the phrase but does not offer any additional verb.

as well as a downward path. You, or if not you, at least the children whom you have brought into the world, for whom you toil, for whom you hoard, for whom you pray, for whom you would give your lives,—they still may be healthy, strong, it may be beautiful, and have all the intellectual and social, as well as the physical advantages, which health, strength, and beauty give."—Ah, why is this divine voice now, as of old, Wisdom crying in the streets, and no man regarding her? I appeal to women, who are initiated, as we men can never be, into the stern mysteries of pain, and sorrow, and self-sacrifice;—they who bring forth children, weep over children, slave for children, and, if they have none of their own, then slave, with the holy instinct of the sexless bee, for the children of others—Let them say, shall this thing be?

4. "THE PERIL IN THE AIR." THE PEPS COMPANY. LEEDS: 1913. REPRODUCED WITH PERMISSION FROM THE WELLCOME TRUST COLLECTION, AVAILABLE AT https://wellcomecollection.org/works/vqz4rf38.

Figure 4. "The Peril in the Air," The Peps Company. Leeds: 1913. (Reproduced with permission from the Wellcome Trust Collection.)

APPENDIX E

VICTORIAN SUBURBANIZATION

Urbanization and suburbanization are integral features of modernizing Victorian society. In Dickens's *Great Expectations* (1861), we see an early treatment of suburban London life as Wemmick shows Pip his "castle" home in Walworth.[1] We include later nineteenth-century examples that suggest the evolution of the suburbs and their residents. George and Weedon Grossmith's *The Diary of a Nobody* (1892) and T.W.H. Crosland's *The Suburbans* (1905) offer satirical portraits of suburban residents that expose their aspirations, egoisms, and follies. Ella Hepworth Dixon's *The Story of a Modern Woman* (1894) is a New Woman novel that illustrates how the suburbs were imagined as a domestic (and presumably safe) site. And the

---

1. See vol. 2, chap. 6 of *Great Expectations*. Walworth is a district of southern London within the Borough of Southwark adjacent to Camberwell.

excerpt from Thomas Runciman's article from *Art Journal* helps us to consider both the architectural design of nineteenth-century suburbs and London's changing geography—a geography that we can study with the selection we include from *Bacon's Library Map of London and Suburbs* (1877). We can use this map to identify prominent locations in Hay's novella and chart the movements of the narrator from London to the suburban area of East Dulwich and back again to the capital.

1. GEORGE AND WEEDON GROSSMITH, FROM *THE DIARY OF A NOBODY* (1892)

We arrived at the Mansion House too early, which was rather fortunate, for I had an opportunity of speaking to his lordship, who graciously condescended to talk with me some minutes; but I must say I was disappointed to find he did not even know Mr. Perkupp, our principal.[2]

I felt as if we had been invited to the Mansion House by one who did not know the Lord Mayor himself. Crowds arrived, and I shall never forget the grand sight. My humble pen can never describe it. I was a little annoyed with Carrie, who kept saying: "Isn't it a pity we don't know anybody?"

2. The characters here are Charles and Caroline (Carrie) Pooter, who have recently moved into a new suburban home at "The Laurels," Brickfield Terrace, Holloway. Mr. Pooter is a City of London clerk with Perkupp's. Mr. Pooter and his wife are honored and extremely excited to attend the ball at the Mansion House. Mansion House: the official residence of the Lord Mayor of London, built in the 1740s.

Once she quite lost her head. I saw someone who looked like Franching, from Peckham, and was moving towards him when she seized me by the coat-tails, and said quite loudly: "Don't leave me," which caused an elderly gentleman, in a court-suit, and a chain round him, and two ladies, to burst out laughing. There was an immense crowd in the supper-room, and, my stars! it was a splendid supper—any amount of champagne.

Carrie made a most hearty supper, for which I was pleased; for I sometimes think she is not strong. There was scarcely a dish she did not taste. I was so thirsty, I could not eat much. Receiving a sharp slap on the shoulder, I turned, and, to my amazement, saw Farmerson, our ironmonger. He said, in the most familiar way: "This is better than Brickfield Terrace, eh?" I simply looked at him, and said coolly: "I never expected to see you here." He said, with a loud, coarse laugh: "I like that—if *you*, why not *me*?" I replied: "Certainly." I wish I could have thought of something better to say. He said: "Can I get your good lady anything?" Carrie said: "No, I thank you," for which I was pleased. I said, by way of reproof to him: "You never sent to-day to paint the bath, as I requested." Farmerson said: "Pardon me, Mr. Pooter, no shop when we're in company, please."

Before I could think of a reply, one of the sheriffs, in full Court costume, slapped Farmerson on the back and hailed him as an old friend, and asked him to dine with him at his lodge. I was astonished. For full five minutes they stood roaring with laughter, and stood digging each other in the ribs. They kept telling each other they didn't look a day older. They began embracing each other and drinking champagne.

To think that a man who mends our scraper should know any member of our aristocracy! I was just moving with Carrie, when Farmerson seized me rather roughly by the collar, and addressing the sheriff, said: "Let me introduce my neighbour, Pooter." He did not even say "Mister." The sheriff handed me a glass of champagne. I felt, after all, it was a great honour to drink a glass of wine with him, and I told him so. We stood chatting for some time, and at last I said: "You must excuse me now if I join Mrs. Pooter." When I approached her, she said: "Don't let me take you away from friends. I am quite happy standing here alone in a crowd, knowing nobody!"

As it takes two to make a quarrel, and as it was neither the time nor the place for it, I gave my arm to Carrie, and said: "I hope my darling little wife will dance with me, if only for the sake of saying we had danced at the Mansion House as guests of the Lord Mayor." Finding the dancing after supper was less formal, and knowing how much Carrie used to admire my dancing in the days gone by, I put my arm round her waist and we commenced a waltz.

A most unfortunate accident occurred. I had got on a new pair of boots. Foolishly, I had omitted to take Carrie's advice; namely, to scratch the soles of them with the points of the scissors or to put a little wet on them. I had scarcely started when, like lightning, my left foot slipped away and I came down, the side of my head striking the floor with such violence that for a second or two I did not know what had happened. I need hardly say that Carrie fell with me with equal violence, breaking the comb in her hair and grazing her elbow.

There was a roar of laughter, which was immediately checked when people found that we had really hurt ourselves. A gentleman assisted Carrie to a seat, and I expressed myself pretty strongly on the danger of having a plain polished floor with no carpet or drugget to prevent people slipping. The gentleman, who said his name was Darwitts, insisted on escorting Carrie to have a glass of wine, an invitation which I was pleased to allow Carrie to accept.

2. THOMAS RUNCIMAN, FROM "LONDON CITY SUBURBS," *ART JOURNAL, 1839–1912* (JUNE 1893): 175–80.

The sinuous walk between Kew Bridge and Isleworth shows the river at its best in shine or shower.[3] The twilights there occasion a lovely greyness never monotonous, for breeze and current are always at work changing the lights and darks. Yet no matter how they shift and alter, the stream is still a soft silver-grey. Until lately, Brentford Ferry was a scene of constant variety and beauty.[4] And though now some factory business has cast its bad shadow around, it is still a suggestive spot, especially in the late summer twilight when earth's solid masses are all warmly dark, while sky and river

3. Kew Bridge crosses the Tideway (upper estuary of the Thames) and links the London Boroughs of Richmond upon Thames and Hounslow. By the late nineteenth century, Kew Bridge experienced significant traffic. Isleworth is a town within the west London Borough of Hounslow.
4. Brentford is a West London suburban town within the Borough of Hounslow. The Brentford Ferry was a traditional means of crossing the Thames to reach the Surrey bank and Kew. It was used to transport cattle and merchandise.

are light—rose or yellow. Isleworth at the same hour is still finer. It arranges into pictures without fudging, looked at either from Richmond way or from below the ferry. Sienna-coloured boats with male and female crews in bright tints of dress, leave silvery dashes every few minutes across the flat olive reflections from the banks. The sedges on both shores, and the eyot close to the ferry,[5] with masts of barges beyond seeming to rise from among its lofty osiers or reeds, make a highly satisfactory scene to the sketcher. Brentford, near at hand, is old and tumbledown—but not too tumbledown—russet-red in its bricks, glittering in its many-sized windows, and full of the unexpected in its chimneys and chimney-pots of all size and every state of unrepair. Close to the same spot is a barge-repairing yard of the richest disorder. Beside the barge, itself all weatherworn red and black paint and rusty stains, orange spars and oars lie around—the countless miscellanea of the carpenters' and smiths' trades. Luxuriant dock leaves and bright green grass decorate the whole place, while hawthorn bushes and loftier trees rise instead of walls enclosing it. It is noteworthy that if you cross the Thames at Hampton and go to Molesey you find nature making different things artistically out of the same material.[6] That is the charm of your London suburbs. You find everything so similar in general character, and yet there come frequent little surprises such as nature only knows how to give.

5. eyot: Small island in a river or lake.
6. Hampton is a suburban London location on the north bank of the Thames in the Borough of Richmond upon Thames. Molesey comprises two towns (East and West Molesey) in the Borough of Elmbridge, Surrey, located on the south bank of the Thames.

3. ELLA HEPWORTH DIXON, FROM *THE STORY OF A MODERN WOMAN* (1894)

And yet she must walk on, get as far away from him as possible.[7] Here, at the North Gate, the slim young poplars detached themselves tremblingly against the pinkish sky, while in front of her stretched the long, white Avenue Road, with its square snug houses, holding themselves aloof in their leafy gardens. She would walk on until she came to Hampstead. Up there, there was space, distance; one's horizon opened out.

* * *

But she was walking alone, steeling her heart against him, in a road in a London suburb. On each side was the prosperous, orderly, contented life of the middle-class, with its placid domesticity, its unemotional joys. From the open window of a long drawing-room came the sound of a young girl's thread-like voice. Upstairs, in the nursery, the lights were already lowered. The white street was deserted. But suddenly from one of the open gateways appeared a pair of sleek chestnuts. The carriage passed out, and as Mary stood waiting at the curb, a man and a woman's smiling faces were photographed on her brain. A prosperous, middle-aged couple, going out to a placid evening's amusement. Then silence again.

7. This brief excerpt from Dixon's novel follows immediately after the protagonist, Mary Erle, refuses Vincent Hemming's proposal to run away with him to start a new life.

On and on, past the Swiss Cottage, the sleepy Tudor College, up Fitzjohn's Avenue with its sham Tudor mansions and its gay little procession of young trees. The girl pushed on, hoping she would tire herself, up the High Street and through a shady road or two, out into the open heath. The after-glow of a crimson sunset still hung in the west. The Surrey Hills were faintly blue, and the heath, with its broken ridges topped with gorse and bracken, swept in superb lines at her feet. The air was very still. Over yonder a mysterious hand had hung a silver sickle in the pale twilight sky.

Mary sank tired on to a seat. But presently two vague figures approached in the growing darkness—the figures of a girl and a young man, working people both, who sat awkwardly down at the other end of the bench, and talked in jerky, constrained whispers. The girl's eyes were bent demurely on her lap, but once, when Mary turned her head in their direction, she could see that the young man's eyes were devouring the face of his shabby little companion with a passionate glance. Something tightened at Mary's throat. Why to-night, of all nights, must she be reminded of what she was giving up? She got up, and began to walk rapidly homeward.

4. T.W.H. CROSLAND, FROM *THE SUBURBANS* (1905)

All the world knows that the suburbans are a people to themselves. Persons of culture, of whom the more respectable quarter of the world is full, have for a generation or so made a point of speaking of the suburbans with hushed voices and a certain contempt. Among the superior class the very word 'suburban' nowadays means a great deal more than it was ever intended to mean. Indeed, though, philologically considered, it is quite an innocent word, with but one meaning, the superior mind has latterly contrived to pack into it meanings enough to start a respectable dictionary. To the superior mind, in fact, 'suburban' is a sort of label which may be properly applied to pretty well everything on the earth that is ill-conditioned, undesirable, and unholy. If a man or a woman have a fault of taste, of inclination, of temperament, of breeding, or even of manner, the superior mind proceeds, on little wings of haste, to pronounce that fault 'suburban.' The whole of the humdrum, platitudinous things of life, all matters and apparatus which, by reason of their frequency, have become somewhat of a bore to the superior person, are wholly and unmitigatedly suburban. It saves time so to dub them, and it soothes the weary heart. Omnibuses, for example, whether green, red, yellow, or otherwise, hurt in their lumbering vulgarity, not to say their utter disrespect for class distinction, every honest, superior soul. To ameliorate the average omnibus, to render it a vehicle of soft and spiritual delights, to rid it of its doubtful plushes, its uncleanly floor, its jogglety garden seats, its bloated driver, and its busybody conductor, were an impossibility.[8] Five miles for twopence cannot be accomplished without certain inconveniently democratic concomitants. You cannot get, at a farthing a mile or under, the immaculate upholsterings, the soft cee-springs, the varnish, the

8. jogglety: moving, unstable, or slightly jolting

exclusiveness, the obsequious touchings of the hat, which are yours by prescriptive right if you keep your own carriage. Hence it comes to pass that a bus, twopenny or penny, offends your delicate spirit, and in sheer unreason, when you ride upon such a rattletrap, you wax wroth and suffer the agonies of the tortured, and out of your martyrdom you cry: 'A plague upon omnibuses! They are suburban!'

5. *BACON'S LIBRARY MAP OF LONDON AND SUBURBS*, SHEET 5, SCALE 9 ⅜ (1877)

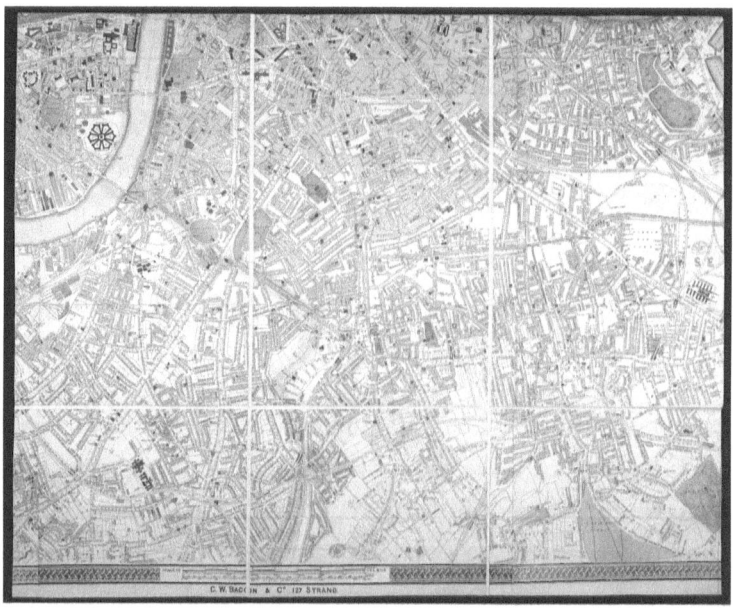

Figure 5. *Bacon's Library Map of London and Suburbs*. (Reproduced with permission from the British Library. [Maps 3480 (241.sheet 5)].)

VISIONS OF THE END

These selections provide insight into how writers in the long nineteenth-century imagined human-environmental interaction and the destructive potential of global-scale forces such as plague, war, and poisonous clouds. In *The Last Man* (1826), Mary Shelley describes an overdetermined end; a mysterious orb darkens the sun as an epidemic ravages the Earth's inhabitants. George Griffiths's speculative battle novel, *The Angel of the Revolution: A Tale of the Coming Terror* (1893), depicts an "Armageddon of the Western World" where "a succession of colossal and unparalleled butcheries" are made possible through technological innovation and war is "waged rather with machinery than with men." An excerpt from M. P. Shiel's *The Purple Cloud* (1901) describes an Arctic adventurer's search for the Pole when he encounters a wandering, toxic "vapour" that expands, "like the smoke of the conflagration of the world," killing humans and animals in its wake. These visions indicate how new understandings of public health, technology, and human impact on the

environment fueled fantasies of both apocalypse and world
(re)making.

1. MARY SHELLEY, FROM *THE LAST MAN* (1826)

The plague had come to Athens. Hundreds of English residents
returned to their own country. Raymond's beloved Athenians,[1]
the free, the noble people of the divinest town in Greece, fell like
ripe corn before the merciless sickle of the adversary. Its pleasant
places were deserted; its temples and palaces were converted into
tombs; its energies, bent before towards the highest objects of
human ambition, were now forced to converge to one point, the
guarding against the innumerous arrows of the plague.

At any other time this disaster would have excited extreme
compassion among us; but it was now passed over, while each
mind was engaged by the coming controversy. It was not so with
me; and the question of rank and right dwindled to insignifi-
cance in my eyes, when I pictured the scene of suffering Athens.[2] I heard of the death of only sons; of wives and husbands
most devoted; of the rending of ties twisted with the heart's

---

1. *The Last Man* adopts features of the roman à clef, and the majority of the
main characters are representations of prominent historical figures, including people close to Mary Shelley. Lord Raymond is an ambitious young
nobleman based on Lord Byron. In the novel, Raymond has left England to
fight on behalf of Greece in its war with Turkey.
2. *The Last Man* is narrated by Lionel Verney (the "last man"), a fictional
representation of Mary Shelley, especially following the death of her hus-
band, Percy Bysshe Shelley.

fibres, of friend losing friend, and young mothers mourning for their first born; and these moving incidents were grouped and painted in my mind by the knowledge of the persons, by my esteem and affection for the sufferers. It was the admirers, friends, fellow soldiers of Raymond, families that had welcomed Perdita to Greece, and lamented with her the loss of her lord, that were swept away, and went to dwell with them in the undistinguishing tomb.[3]

The plague at Athens had been preceded and caused by the contagion from the East; and the scene of havoc and death continued to be acted there, on a scale of fearful magnitude. A hope that the visitation of the present year would prove the last, kept up the spirits of the merchants connected with these countries; but the inhabitants were driven to despair, or to a resignation which, arising from fanaticism, assumed the same dark hue. America had also received the taint; and, were it yellow fever or plague, the epidemic was gifted with a virulence before unfelt. The devastation was not confined to the towns, but spread throughout the country; the hunter died in the woods, the peasant in the corn-fields, and the fisher on his native waters.

A strange story was brought to us from the East, to which little credit would have been given, had not the fact been attested by a multitude of witnesses, in various parts of the world. On the twenty-first of June, it was said that an hour before noon, a black sun arose: an orb, the size of that luminary, but dark, defined, whose beams were shadows, ascended from the west; in about an

---

3. Perdita is Lionel's sister and Raymond's wife.

hour it had reached the meridian, and eclipsed the bright parent of day. Night fell upon every country, night, sudden, rayless, entire. The stars came out, shedding their ineffectual glimmerings on the light-widowed earth. But soon the dim orb passed from over the sun, and lingered down the eastern heaven. As it descended, its dusky rays crossed the brilliant ones of the sun, and deadened or distorted them. The shadows of things assumed strange and ghastly shapes. The wild animals in the woods took fright at the unknown shapes figured on the ground. They fled they knew not whither; and the citizens were filled with greater dread, at the convulsion which "shook lions into civil streets;"[4]—birds, strong-winged eagles, suddenly blinded, fell in the market-places, while owls and bats shewed themselves welcoming the early night. Gradually the object of fear sank beneath the horizon, and to the last shot up shadowy beams into the otherwise radiant air. Such was the tale sent us from Asia, from the eastern extremity of Europe, and from Africa as far west as the Golden Coast.

Whether this story were true or not, the effects were certain. Through Asia, from the banks of the Nile to the shores of the Caspian, from the Hellespont even to the sea of Oman, a sudden panic was driven. The men filled the mosques; the women, veiled, hastened to the tombs, and carried offerings to the dead, thus to preserve the living. The plague was forgotten, in this new fear which the black sun had spread; and, though the dead multiplied, and the streets of Ispahan, of Pekin, and of Delhi were

4. From William Shakespeare, *Antony and Cleopatra*, act 5, scene 1.

strewed with pestilence-struck corpses, men passed on, gazing on the ominous sky, regardless of the death beneath their feet.[5] The christians sought their churches,—christian maidens, even at the feast of roses, clad in white, with shining veils, sought, in long procession, the places consecrated to their religion, filling the air with their hymns; while, ever and anon, from the lips of some poor mourner in the crowd, a voice of wailing burst, and the rest looked up, fancying they could discern the sweeping wings of angels, who passed over the earth, lamenting the disasters about to fall on man.

In the sunny clime of Persia, in the crowded cities of China, amidst the aromatic groves of Cashmere, and along the southern shores of the Mediterranean, such scenes had place.[6] Even in Greece the tale of the sun of darkness encreased [*sic*] the fears and despair of the dying multitude. We, in our cloudy isle, were far removed from danger, and the only circumstance that brought these disasters at all home to us, was the daily arrival of vessels from the east, crowded with emigrants, mostly English; for the Moslems, though the fear of death was spread keenly among them, still clung together; that, if they were to die (and if they were, death would as readily meet them on the homeless sea, or in far England, as in Persia,)—if they were to die, their bones might rest in earth made sacred by the relics of true believers. Mecca had never before been so crowded with pilgrims; yet the

5. Ispahan: Isfahan, major city in central Iran; Pekin: Beijing, now capital city in China; Delhi: city in northern India.
6. Cashmere: Anglicization of Kashmir.

Arabs neglected to pillage the caravans, but, humble and weaponless, they joined the procession, praying Mahomet to avert plague from their tents and deserts.

2. GEORGE GRIFFITH, FROM *THE ANGEL OF THE REVOLUTION: A TALE OF THE COMING TERROR* (1893)

CHAPTER XXXVIII
The Beginning of the End

IT is now time to return to Britain, to the land which the course of events had so far appeared to single out as the battle-ground upon which was to be fought the Armageddon of the Western World—that conflict of the giants, the issue of which was to decide whether the Anglo-Saxon race was still to remain in the forefront of civilisation and progress, or whether it was to fall, crushed and broken, beneath the assaults of enemies descending upon the motherland of the Anglo-Saxon nations; whether the valour and personal devotion, which for a thousand years had scarcely known a defeat by flood or field, was still to pursue its course of victory, or whether it was to succumb to weight of numbers and mechanical discipline, reinforced by means of assault and destruction which so far had turned the world-war of 1904 into a succession of colossal and unparalleled butcheries, such as had never been known before in the history of human strife.

When the Allied fleets, bearing the remains of the British and German armies which had been driven out of the Netherlands, reached England, and the news of the crowning disaster of the war in Europe was published in detail in the newspapers, the popular mind seemed suddenly afflicted with a paralysis of stupefaction.

Men looked back over the long series of triumphs in which British valour and British resolution had again and again proved themselves invulnerable to the assaults of overwhelming numbers. They thought of the glories of the Peninsula, of the unbreakable strength of the thin red line at Waterloo, of the magnificent madness of Balaclava, and the invincible steadiness and discipline that had made Inkermann a word to be remembered with pride as long as the English name endured.[7]

Then their thoughts reverted to the immediate past, and they heard the shock of colossal armaments, compared with which the armies of the past appeared but pigmies in strength. They saw empires defended by millions of soldiers crushed in a few weeks, and a wave of conquest sweep in one unbroken roll from end to end of a continent in less time than it would have taken Napoleon or Wellington to have fought a single campaign. Huge fortresses, rendered, as men had believed, impregnable by the employment of every resource known to the most advanced

7. Peninsula: Griffith refers to the Peninsular War (1807–1814), or the conflict fought by Spain, Portugal, and Great Britain on the Iberian Peninsula against Napoleon's forces. Balaclava: Battle of Balaklava (October 25, 1854) during the Crimean War, part of the Siege of Sevastopol (1854–1855); Inkermann: the Battle of Inkermann (November 5, 1854) was a battle of the Crimean War fought by the British and French against the Russian imperial army.

military science, had been reduced to heaps of defenceless ruins in a few hours by a bombardment, under which their magnificent guns had lain as impotent as though they had been the culverins of three hundred years ago.

It seemed like some hideous nightmare of the nations, in which Europe had gone mad, revelling in superhuman bloodshed and destruction,—a conflict in which more than earthly forces had been let loose, accomplishing a carnage so immense that the mind could only form a dim and imperfect conception of it. And now this red tide of desolation had swept up to the western verge of the Continent, and was there gathering strength and volume day by day against the hour when it should burst and oversweep the narrow strip of water which separated the inviolate fields of England from the blackened and blood-stained waste that it had left behind it from the Russian frontier to the German Ocean.

It seemed impossible, and yet it was true. The first line of defence, the hitherto invincible fleet, magnificently as it had been managed, and heroically as it had been fought, had failed in the supreme hour of trial. It had failed, not because the sailors of Britain had done their duty less valiantly than they had done in the days of Rodney and Nelson,[8] but simply because the conditions of naval warfare had been entirely changed, because the personal equation had been almost eliminated from the problem

8. Vice-Admiral Horatio Nelson (1758–1805), legendary British naval commander of multiple campaigns and battles, including the Battle of Trafalgar (1805). Admiral George Brydges Rodney (1718–1792), usually remembered for his commands during the American War of Independence.

of battle, and because the new warfare of the seas had been waged rather with machinery than with men.

3. M. P. SHIEL, FROM *THE PURPLE CLOUD* (1901)

I had started from the Pole with a well-filled sledge, and the sixteen dogs left alive from the ice-packing which buried my comrades. This was on the evening of the 13th April. I had saved from the wreck of our things most of the whey-powder, pemmican, &c., as well as the theodolite, compass, chronometer, train-oil lamp for cooking, and other implements:[9] I was therefore in no doubt as to my course, and I had provisions for ninety days. But ten days from the start my supply of dog-food failed, and I had to begin to slaughter my only companions, one by one.

Well, in the third week the ice became horribly rough, and with moil and toil enough to wear a bear to death, I did only five miles a day. After the day's work I would crawl with a dying sigh into the sleeping-bag, clad still in the load of skins which stuck to me a mere filth of grease, to sleep the sleep of a swine, indifferent if I never woke.

Always—day after day—on the south-eastern horizon, brooded sullenly that curious stretched-out region of purple vapour, like the smoke of the conflagration of the world. And I noticed that its length constantly reached out and out, and silently grew.

9. theodolite: optical instrument used for measuring angles between visible points, traditionally used for surveying and meteorology; chronometer: accurate timepiece used for maritime navigation.

* * *

Once I had a very pleasant dream. I dreamed that I was in a garden—an Arabian paradise—so sweet was the perfume. All the time, however, I had a sub-consciousness of the gale which was actually blowing from the S.E. over the ice, and, at the moment when I awoke, was half-wittedly droning to myself; 'It is a Garden of Peaches; but I am not really in the garden: I am really on the ice; only, the S.E. storm is wafting to me the aroma of this Garden of Peaches.'

I opened my eyes—I started—I sprang to my feet! For, of all the miracles!—I could not doubt—an actual aroma like peach-blossom *was* in the algid air about me!

Before I could collect my astonished senses, I began to vomit pretty violently, and at the same time saw some of the dogs, mere skeletons as they were, vomiting, too. For a long time I lay very sick in a kind of daze, and, on rising, found two of the dogs dead, and all very queer. The wind had now changed to the north.

Well, on I staggered, fighting every inch of my deplorably weary way. This odour of peach-blossom, my sickness, and the death of the two dogs, remained a wonder to me.

Two days later, to my extreme mystification (and joy), I came across a bear and its cub lying dead at the foot of a hummock. I could not believe my eyes. There she lay on her right side, a spot of dirty-white in a disordered patch of snow, with one little eye open, and her fierce-looking mouth also; and the cub lay across her haunch, biting into her rough fur. I set to work upon her, and allowed the dogs a glorious feed on the blubber, while I myself had a great banquet on the fresh meat. I had to leave the greater part of the two carcasses, and I can feel again now the hankering reluctance—quite unnecessary, as it turned out—with which I trudged onwards. Again and again I found myself asking: 'Now, what could have killed those two bears?'

With brutish stolidness I plodded ever on, almost like a walking machine, sometimes nodding in sleep while I helped the dogs, or manœuvred the sledge over an ice-ridge, pushing or pulling. On the 3rd June, a month and a half from my start, I took an observation with the theodolite, and found that I was not yet 400 miles from the Pole, in latitude 84° 50'. It was just as though some Will, some Will, was obstructing and retarding me.

However, the intolerable cold was over, and soon my clothes no longer hung stark on me like armour. Pools began to appear in the ice, and presently, what was worse, my God, long lanes, across which, somehow, I had to get the sledge. But about the same time all fear of starvation passed away: for on the 6th June I came across another dead bear, on the 7th three, and thenceforth, in rapidly growing numbers, I met not bears only, but fulmars, guillemots, snipes, Ross's gulls, little awks [*sic*]—all, all, lying dead on the ice. And never anywhere a living thing, save me, and the two remaining dogs.

If ever a poor man stood shocked before a mystery, it was I now. I had a big fear on my heart.

www.ingramcontent.com/pod-product-compliance
Lightning Source LLC
Chambersburg PA
CBHW020613030726
47497CB00007B/2216